VERA'S ALIEN LEADER

DEDICATION

To all my closeted monster lovers and the
friends you've converted.

BOOK - MA

This book is intended for mature audiences for adult language, sexual content, and violence. It deals with themes of addiction, gambling, SA, miscarriage, first contact, and religion.

VÒLLØÃIAN GLOSSARY

ĜHA: PARTNER WHO MAKES MY SECOND HEART BEAT, OR SOULMATE

ĜHAJO: PLURAL OF ĜHA

JÈ: YES

G'Ú: NO

D'O GO CHU MERCHU: MY ENERGY IS YOURS

JISA: AN ANATOMICAL SHEILD THAT PROTECTS THE SKIN

HØ: CHILD

LUSHI: A THOUSAND NONDESCRIPT MEASURES

ROSHEV: A GAME PLAYED ON SHOJO WITH CARVED CHIPS

ĠÌ: ANIMAL OR CREATURE

B'OSHIPHI: AN INSTRUMENT SIMILAR TO A GUITAR

RERU: AN INSTRUMENT SIMILAR TO A HARMONICA

SÀ: BEAUTIFUL, REMINISCENT OF NATURE

ŜŒḦŮ: SMALL FURRY CREATURES WITH USELESS FURRY WINGS

YUE'E: A DRAGONOID THAT LIVES IN A CAVE

PRONUNCIATION GUIDE

ĜHA: SAID LIKE "AHH," A PLEASING SIGH

ĜHAJO: AHD - JAY

PEHOLOE: PAY - HOE - LOW

CHARACTER NAMES

VERA OKSANA: VEH-RUH OHK-SAH-NUH
ASTON ANDREWS: AS-TUHN AN-DROOZ
ROXIE HOLT: RAHK-SEE HOHLT
ALBA REYNOLDS: AHL-BUH REH-NUHLDZ
BLOSSOM: BLAH-SUHM
KANO TISUGO D'ERUROGESHU: KAH-NOH TEE-SOO-GOH
DEH-ROO-ROH-GEH-SHOO
KETHI ROGESHU: KEH-THEE ROH-GEH-SHOO
LIRO SHEHO: LEE-ROH SHEH-HOH
NOHKTIR SHEHO: NOX-TEER SHEH-HOH
LLAZHO TITUVO: YAH-ZHOH TEE-TOO-VOH
RIHU TISUGO: REE-HOO TEE-SOO-GOH
ROYI TISUGO: ROY-EE TEE-SOO-GOH
ZHU: ZHOO
GOWI: GOH-WEE
HOGA: HOH-GAH
JIGU: JEE-GOO
PA: PAH
RRA: RRAH
SOEKHO: SOEX-OH
ZHALISEE: ZHAH-LEE-SEE

CHAPTER ONE

Vera

I let my cards speak for me. My hand looks beautiful, laid out on the table like that. Ace, king, queen, jack, and the ten of diamonds – sparkling like my pile of winnings and the metallic steel card holding my tickets to space. It's a royal flush. Winning never felt so good. The universe must be on my side.

Before my opponent can call for another round he can't afford, I gather my mish-mashed rewards. After retiring from professional poker, I would say I know when to fold. Mr. Meat-Fist's hands curl in fury at my cheeky grin. He must not have known about me. Nor does he get the chance to find out when a pretty server swings by the table at the right time, seemingly oblivious to the tension I caused. She leans over my favorite loser to offer her ample bosom and a tray of drinks. I duck behind her and out of the old bar. I only wished I'd left the man enough money to gift the girl a nice tip or cab fare for his ride home.

When I'm a mile down the road, I smile to myself. I hadn't intended to con the man out of his tickets. I even told him I used to play poker professionally – but he underestimated me. He assumed a pretty girl like me with blue doe eyes and platinum blonde hair couldn't *play* anyone. Initially, I'd made enough money to retire in my first year of professional games, but I still played for the full five years I promised myself I would. Over time, it transitioned from being about the money to being about the thrill. It was fun to bet on Lady Luck sometimes and see my risks pay off. I liked the excitement of the game and how it felt like an adventure. Crappy games in crappy little bars usually weren't enough to pump my blood. But that familiar adrenaline rush coursed through my veins when Big Man offered his infamous little card, holding coveted *SS Herculean* tickets.

It carried me all the way home. Where, Ralph, a crotchety old man with a penchant for Marlboros, waved at me before he buzzed me through to the penthouse. He was so unapproachable; I could never understand why the building hired him. Then, one night, a crazy ex came through swinging around a gun and shouting to see some dude named Jason. Ralph took one step out from the desk, gave the girl a look of disdain, and asked her to leave. She did. From then on, I didn't question Ralph or the building's choice. Plus, it wasn't like he had ever treated me poorly. He was just gruff.

The pleasant *ding* of the elevator let me know I'd reached my sky-high oasis. A penthouse apartment was my first purchase when I finally earned big money. Before, I lived in a shared studio with a stripper named Violet and her two cats. She had a habit of being late on rent and an unstable boyfriend who would bang on our door at two in the morning asking to bone down. Otherwise, she was nice enough. She had a bigger chest than me and pouty, filled lips. We worked at the same bar, and the customers loved her. Still, I wasn't sad to say goodbye.

I kick off my chucks next to the door and pad across the faux-fur rug lining my foyer. The apartment opens into exactly what you would imagine a penthouse to look like. A modern kitchen with shiny, flush cabinets and chrome details sits to the left, while a white leather sectional designates a living room to the right. My bare feet pad up the cool glass stairs behind the couch to the loft, where the master bedroom holds a bed big enough for ten people. I duck into my closet and toss my black zipper hoodie in my "wear-again" bin. Then, I drag out my old luggage and fill it with the outfits I want to wear in space while dialing my best friend's number.

"You've reached Aston Andrews." She answers in her customer-service voice. I put the phone on speaker and set it on one of my closet shelves.

"Pack your bags, Ace. We're going to space."

With a rich girl's name like Aston Andrews and a family-fortune to match, my best friend needed a nickname for the seedy places I frequented. Thus, Ace was created. In poker, Ace had the highest value. In my life, Aston held the same. Sure, everyone in the area would know her face alone, but it helped her to step into her alter ego. Aston was the face of multi-billion-dollar enterprises. Ace was the girl who could outdrink and outfight your best guy any night of the week.

"Sorry, I'm not sure I heard you right." Her phone clicks and her voice becomes less clear, letting me know she's on speaker, "Did you say space? Like in the movie *Love Amongst the Stars* space?"

"Yup. Endless, dark, star-speckled space."

I hear the thud of her own luggage and the muffled sound of a zipper. Her sigh comes closer to the receiver, then, "What do you even wear in space?"

"Let me check."

Scrolling through *SS Herculean*'s webpage on my phone, I learn that the ship is like a cruise liner, but instead of the ocean, we get to party in the vast, wide-open wasteland of space. There would be dinners and entertainment, educational tours, cocktail hours, and so much more. The ship was outfitted with an entire water theme park, a zero-gravity laser tag rink, and an adult bar and casino. It even bragged that real astronauts would supervise spacewalks in the future.

"How many swimsuits do you think are too many?" She asks, and I can only imagine her excitement as she tries to narrow down her collection. My own excitement ate at my veins with each piece I packed. My feminine urge to plan for the experience I *thought* I would have had well and truly taken over.

Looking through my suitcase, I count the colorful strings and straps, "I've packed ten. It's a fourteen-day trip, though. So conceptually, you could bring more."

"Do you think sunglasses on a space yacht is tacky?"

I look at the Ray-Bans I threw in my suitcase and consider taking them out. "No, the sun is still bright there."

For about an hour, we talked and packed. Then, we second-guess our packing skills and talk while repacking – doublechecking for underwear, socks, and a dress good enough to make an alien fall in love. Even though we earthlings still hadn't had first contact. When we both are satisfied that we won't miss a photo-op in space, I walk Aston through the check-in process and tell her to meet me at the gate in the morning.

Dragging my bags beside the door, I recheck the information. Then, I turn in for the night. I will board the indestructible, first-ever commercial hyperdrive ship tomorrow morning. The *SS Herculean*. Me, my best friend, and nearly five-hundred other humans who want to experience deep space would be on board, and I couldn't wait.

CHAPTER TWO

Space was the coolest. The first day, I felt like a kid in a candy store. I wanted to do everything and visit every activity. I couldn't decide between Shuffleboard or the space lecture movie from the company's CEO. Luckily, Aston was happy to make the decisions, dragging us to the exciting activities. We watched the entirety of the Alien franchise in space last night. And today, we were going to the on-deck fortune teller.

Honestly, I thought fortune tellers were a little bit gimmicky. I was the kind of girl who built my own luck and worked for my wins. But Aston loved that kind of stuff. She was always going on about that rich dude's quote about billionaires using astrology. Her company even had an astrologist on staff. So, when she told me it would be "so fun," how could I resist?

A woman in a tailored navy jumpsuit popped her head up behind the counter when the bell tapped against the door upon our arrival. The counter was covered in spacy knickknacks for purchase. Little moons and astrological signs on keychains. Crystal stickers and glass bottles filled with colorful rocks. Aston turned her back to the rest of the room, more than happy to converse with Madam Indigo about the services we wanted today while I looked around.

I expected to enter a tiny room in the ship dripping with purple velvet curtains and poor lighting. Instead, I was brought to a tiny room with a massive porthole overlooking the vast expanse of space. Even though I'd seen the view a dozen times, it never ceased to take my breath away. The sheer immensity of it all made me feel so much smaller. I was a mere drop in the universe. The view made all my Earth problems seem inconsequential in the grand scheme.

Aston tapped me on the shoulder, pointing to the tiny circular reading table. Beyond it, glow lights nurtured a line of plants on a clean metallic shelf. To the left, jars with various dried herbs were stacked inside a glass-doored cabinet. An altar decorated with black and white candles and a bowl of herbs sat below.

"Everything is glued down," Madam Indigo tells me, noticing my close inspection. "You never know what can happen in space, right?"

She motions for us to join her at the table, and I stop snooping to participate. Aston and I share the faux leather pouf across from Madam Indigo as she pulls a silken cloth from the table. Black and silver tarot cards are revealed, fanned out in our direction.

"Think of your question and point to the card, or cards, you are most drawn to."

I let Aston go first, watching her close her eyes and move her finger along the circle's edge. Her head is tilted back, her lips pursed in concentration, and it doesn't take a medium to know the basis of her question. Aston wants to know if she's going to find love. Of course, she would never ask her regular astrologer this question because that was a business relationship. But, here, in space, it was free game.

Aston had worked really hard on her business lately, proving to her father and brothers that she could do nontraditional work and still make it in the world. She did it too. Aston had built an incredible art business, selling her works among a dozen other creatives at her highbrow gallery. She built it from scratch, started on social media and at networking events without ever dropping the Andrews' name. But Aston wanted someone to share it with. She wanted to be with someone who would tell her they were proud of her because she did the impossible. She wanted someone to share her life experiences with.

6

No matter how proud of her I was, she stood on the side of my opinion, being biased because I would love anything she did. She wasn't wrong, but I still didn't think she needed a man to tell her otherwise. She deserved to validate herself. But if it would make her happy, it would make me happy.

Madam Indigo pulled the card Aston pointed at, plus two others. Laying them on the table, face up, her feathered eyebrows pinch together. Then, she interprets them for my friend.

"It seems you want a love that feels all-encompassing and serious. And it seems like you will have that. The kind of love coming into your life won't be exactly what you expect," She taps the center card before pointing to the last one. "But it will be what you need and will change you indefinitely.

"It will be important that you remain open-minded in this endeavor. You are the kind of person who knows what they want and has learned their lessons on fighting against the universe's wishes. Don't forget those things."

Aston nods and doesn't press Madam Indigo for more. Instead, she turns and motions to me to get my reading. I have no clue what to ask, but it turns out that it doesn't matter. As Madam Indigo shuffles the cards carefully, staring into my eyes as she goes, a card flies from the deck, landing face-up on the table. Madam Indigo's memorable eyebrows shoot up. She tries to shuffle down her cards again, and the other slides out of the deck into her lap. I point to the card at the top of the deck for my third.

"Spirit obviously has something to tell you," The fortuneteller muses. I return her curious grin with a tight smile. Death is my first card. I glance over at Aston, and she gives me an encouraging nod. Then, I turn to face Madam Indigo.

"Many people fear that card," She starts, pointing to the silver skull embossed on the matte black paper. "But it is generally very metaphorical."

If her words are meant to be a comfort, they do not work. *'Generally'* is not a word I want to hear when dealing with the occult. If Madam Indigo feels the shift in my energy, she doesn't voice it. She continues her reading.

"What is more interesting are the cards that follow. Yes, you will experience a significant life change. I feel it concerns your environment, but I can't be sure. But then, you come into this time of ease and flow. You go into a time when the rewards of this change become apparent. Until you master the transformation and find yourself in a place of leadership, where you will be asked to work collaboratively. A place where you will help others and comfort them through the change surrounding them.

"This is a positive reading," She confirms, staring into my eyes. I nod, mumble some form of thanks, and then stand from the table. I'm waiting by the counter, ready to pay, and Aston chats with Madam Indigo and thanks her profusely. All the while, my mind churns on what kind of metaphorical death I'll need to experience.

My life on Earth is finally stable. After years of fighting to leave the conditions of my childhood behind, I didn't want to make any more major changes. I loved my environment. I loved my life. Sure, I needed a thrill occasionally, but this trip to space would carry me through for months, maybe even years. I pulled out my wallet and felt my lucky poker deck fall to the floor. Leaving my card on the counter, I tuck the box back into my pocket. Aston pays for my reading and tugs me out the door.

"You didn't have to be so rude to Madam Indigo just because tarot and astrology aren't your things."

8

Her reprimand is said in a kind tone, and I nod noncommittally. I muttered an apology to Aston, and that seemed to work. Her shoulders relax, but mine won't budge.

One of the ship staff walks by with a tray of sparkly blue drinks in martini glasses, and I say, "I think that's what I need."

Aston smiles, "Now, you're speaking my language."

By the time we go to bed, I've forgotten all about the sketchy tarot reading. All I cared about now was dancing under the starlight until my feet ached and sharing the pure joy of this experience with my closest friend.

CHAPTER THREE

It had been a week on the most beautiful, futuristic dream boat I'd ever seen when the other shoe dropped. The initial launch was like riding a roller coaster; the United Nations Space Station was phenomenal, and seeing the *SS Herculean* for the first time made my heart pound double-time. Since boarding, Aston and I had spent every waking moment looking out portholes, drinking our fill of alcohol, and partying with some of the truly wealthy members on board. We explored every public inch of the ship and used the itinerary to plan the rest of our days. They would be jam-packed with the best activities. We were heading to adult-only laser tag this morning when the captain announced it was time for the hyperdrive jump.

He assured everyone it would be a smooth ride, though he recommended we find the nearest safety seat and look away from the portholes. Two seats were available along the outer wall of the hallway we currently traversed. Aston and I were excited, practically bouncing in our seats as the countdown went off. A staff member came by to offer us a drink, and Aston accepted on behalf of both of us. I held on to my seat straps. Even with the security of the X-straps, it felt like my stomach dropped from the unnatural speed. Light flashed brightly against the ship's metallic walls, and then my heart crumpled as the sound of shearing metal and screeching alarms began.

Aston dropped her drinks to the floor, choosing to hold onto her seat as turbulence hit the *SS Herculean*. More shearing and a sound reminiscent of crunching cans hit as the ship is torn to the left. I slam back into the seat when a staffer in full space gear signals through a crunchy-sounding radio for us to follow her to a safety pod.

My fingers tremble as I click the button on my belt, watching the fabric slither away. I keep close to the wall, helping Aston as I glance back in the direction the staffer is headed. She jogs around a corner only moments before another bang sends us against the opposite wall. A loud sound, like a vacuum seal, sounds around the corner. When we catch up with the staffer, all we see is a big metal wall in the way. The lights in the corridor flicker out momentarily, and Aston screams, clawing onto my arm. I keep still, holding my fear inside as the adrenaline finally catches up to the catastrophe. Red lights flicker along the hallway floors, bathing the metallic walls in a horrific rosy hue. Following the blinking lights, we head in the opposite direction before entering a safety corridor and walking further through the ship. Sealed doors slip shut behind us with increasingly frightening thumps, but we keep walking.

Aston shakes like a leaf, and I'm confident her nails have drawn blood, but I can't tell in the red light. The new corridor does nothing to soothe my nerves as the blaring alarms continue. When we finally reach the safe destination, all I see is absolute chaos. About a hundred people are gathered in front of three doors ringed in blue light. Men shout, waving around money clips and begging the personnel to let them into one of the rooms. Here, the captain's repeated mayday messages come in surround sound.

"This is the SS. Herculean *three warp-jumps from Earth requesting emergency response. Please respond."* The captain crackles. Children scream as another impact hits, and we are all tossed sideways. A baby cries and screams somewhere, and mothers cling tight to their kids. I realize there are two other doors at both ends, already sealed shut. Sliding my hand into Aston's, I pull us forward through the mob to hear what the officials are saying. It's worse than I could have imagined.

The guard's eyes betray his panic, but he stands tall and blocks the entrance to the escape pod behind him. This guy is clearly uncomfortable. His shirt collar digs into the throbbing vein in his neck, and his teeth are clenched as the screaming aristocrat yells in his face. The one-percenter cocks back an arm, throwing a punch at the stoic guard. Knocking away the man's fist, the guard growls through gritted teeth, "The escape pods can only support ten people for five days. After that, we may not even need to evacuate. So please step back, sir. Women and children will be the first priority at the captain's command."

Aston cries beside me now. She's put together the same thing I have. If we have to evacuate, fifty people are not five hundred. It's not even enough space for the children. If a rescue ship is unable to reach us, if we're unable to finish this journey – No. I don't let myself think about it. Instead, I think about how we can get organized and how I can help this situation. My best friend lets out a hiccupping sob beside me, and I turn to start with her.

"Aston, honey, look at me," I command, crouching the half-foot that I need to put myself in her eye line. Her green eyes are watery and shiny as they flick open. Tears gather along her bottom row of thick lashes, and I remind myself to keep my emotions in check. Until proven otherwise, this panic is a complete bluff. Then, when her eyes are solidly locked on mine, I explain, "They're bluffing, Aston. The ship has safety precautions for this. We saw them ourselves. As long as we don't keep hitting space rocks, the ship is in mostly working order."

She nods, sniffling wetly. Still, her hands cling to mine, claws in my palms like she's gripping a lifeline. I pull one hand away, brush away a tear, and nod at her again.

"This is good. This means we can wait for the next ship to come through and help us." I wait for her to nod again, "I need you to put on your big girl panties, Ace. We need to help the guards gain control. Because the ship might not be an immediate issue, but if things escalate here, we could be in the hunger games real quick, you hear me?"

She nods again, but her eyes are still glazed. She keeps those eyes on me and carefully releases my shaking hands. Finally, I give her a command that will be easy to follow, "Get all the kids together and put them right in front of the guards."

I don't tell her I will take care of the parents or let the guards handle any major hotheads. She repeats my command back to me and then searches for children. The alarms still scream, and people stream in from various safety corridors behind me. The ship's captain still sends out support requests every few minutes. I talk to a pair of guards in front of one of the red-rimmed doors first.

"Is there any way we can shut off the blaring here?" My question must be shocking because the guard's brows pinch together in confusion. "It's loud. It's scaring the children and guests. If we get the sound off in this room, we might be able to de-escalate the situation a little."

Luckily, guard number one's companion reaches for their radio. I realized then that they were probably grateful I wasn't trying to get on the sealed pod. The radio in guard two's hand crackles to life as she repeats my question into the device. A staticky response comes, and relief washes through me.

"First mate to Stevens, deactivating alarms in the pod-loading deck. All holes are sealed, and emergency assistance is being requested."

It only takes a moment for the sound to end, and the entire room goes quiet. Until one loud-mouthed elitist shouts, "What is the meaning of this?"

The murmurs of the crowd pick up once again, and chaos ensues. Luckily, I got really good at gaining the attention of brawlers before I was a poker player. Sticking my thumb and forefinger into my mouth, I whistle loudly. Heads swivel towards me, and I catch Aston in the crowd, gathering a little group of children by the doors.

"Listen up!" I shout, ignoring the hundreds of sets of panicked eyes on me. "Mothers, get your children to the front of the room. My girl Aston over there wants them front and center at each available escape pod door. Mommas, you all are right behind them. All of you men who helped procreate those children behind your ladies. Anyone else behind them. I want three equal lines."

Some people look to the guards, who nod in agreement with me taking over, indicating where the lines could begin. Aston keeps moving through the crowd, helping the children and their mothers toward the front. The first moment of peace rolls through the crowd. Sure, a couple of the men are furious. They can't believe they won't be on one of these escape pods. With my best lying skills, I tell them that there are more. They're below the ship, waiting for the first five to drop. It seems to work because the best lies are the ones you want to believe.

Soon enough, the captain's emergency request messages stopped repeating over the stereo. Instead, great news spreads throughout the chamber, "All ship damages have been repaired. Ship is stable. We have navigated the remainder of the asteroid belt. Thank you for your cooperation. Emergency evacuation protocol has ended. Lunch will be served on the Skydeck in an hour."

The sound of the inconvenienced rich fills the room as the men file back through the corridors. Mothers cry in relief, clinging to their kids with bright, shining smiles. One woman to my left beams at her little girl brightly. Crouched beside the curly-haired tot, the woman asks, "Should we have ice cream for lunch? I think we should have ice cream for lunch."

The child is enthusiastically in agreement as they stand to shuffle back into the main sectors of the ship. Aston waves at the little kids as they head toward the doors before collapsing into my outstretched arms. Her words are muffled against the fabric of my shirt as she grumbles, "I'm not built to navigate this kind of trauma."

Ditto. Instead of joining her pity party, I hugged her tight. I'm relieved and grateful that we're not dead in space right now. I'm especially happy that she's okay. I don't know how I would ever forgive myself if I invited her on this trip and we didn't make it home. Giving her one last comforting squeeze, I realize most of the people have made it out of the evacuation chamber. The cute little curly-haired tike and her beautiful mother are near the back of the crowd, nearing the door.

When the door slams closed in front of them and the alarms blare again, I can't manage to keep the fear and panic off my face. All my guards were down, and I didn't want to die.

CHAPTER FOUR
Kano

Two and a Half Moons Ago

Kneeling in the crumbles of an ashen crystal, I pray, "Vova, please grant me a *ĝha*."

It has been my prayer for five turns of Shojo. Ever since the Death of Baso Sheva, when all our women suffered in the goddess's image, I pray. My tribe needs more women so we can have more families, so they can adventure further and discover more of Shojo's abundance. Still, I think to put myself first. I could tell you it is because I am their leader and need to model the proper behavior, but it would be a lie. I put myself first because I am lonely. I wish to have both my hearts beat in tandem and feel my blood strengthen inside me. This is why I pray she brings me a *ĝha* and maybe some for my men. I wish for her to bless our village again. Then, I laid myself at her mercy and expressed my gratitude before ending my prayer.

"D'o go chu merchu, Baso Sheva."

My *jisa* alerts me to Rihu's arrival before he does, and I instantly shoot to my feet. He is shorter than I am but no less a warrior. His horns curve differently than mine, and where my skin is a dark emerald color and my markings like liquid silver, his is like the *loki* brush, lighter and cooler, with darker green markings. We may both be Tisugo, but our differences do not stop there. He and Royi have one another, and Rihu's mother, Jaye, still lives. Even with the lack of *ĝhajo*, they are content with their family. Both Riho and Royi have few worries.

"Kano! The *peholoe* are looking for you." He says, bouncing back and forth on his bare toes, looking toward the torrential sky island. I withhold my groan, brushing the spiky crystalline pieces from my linen pants. *What could they possibly want?*

"Many blessings, Rihu," I say, walking past him onto the path. The further into Wupeso I get, the more worried I become. Usually, the *peholoe* seek me out. This is because they are annoying, and as much as I love each and every one of the elders, I have more important things to do than let them play with my hair. Still, I climb the stairs carved into the karst. My mount, Lewe, glides on the draft beside me, ruffling his feathers when he lands on one of the island's many ledges. *Showoff.*

The *peholoe* all live together in a sprawling bungalow buried in the trees. The jungles of the karsts and floating islands are denser than the trees on the ground, and some people prefer to build homes in their expansive heights. This isn't the case for the *peholoe.* They simply enjoy being above everyone else.

I follow a slight incline of planks upward to the base floor. Here, the elders sit on woven mats around little bark chips they've carved with runes and use to fill their days. The adventure never ends for the *peholoe.*

"Kano!" Pa exclaims, dropping his chips face-up and forfeiting his place in their game. Pa is younger than the others, but he aged much faster when he lost his *ĝha.* His decline was only natural without the strength of a second heart beating.

The game quickly dissipates upon my arrival as Jigu, Hoga, Gowi, and Rra all join Pa in greeting me. Jigu is the quickest of the bunch. She is also surprisingly strong. She nimbly pulls me down to meet her and locks her sea-green horns with mine before patting a hand on my chest and stepping away. She motions for Hoga to do the same, but Hoga has never been a tangler. Instead, the pointed spade of her tail flicks in greeting, and her wise eyes narrow in my direction.

Since Hoga didn't want a tangle, Gowi took her place. The tallest of the *peholoe*, she meets me eye to eye when our horns tangle, and she always waits for a beat too long before unlocking our horns. She drags her horn against mine as she detaches, and I feel my skin cool icily around my cheeks. I rub a hand over the sharp tip of my horn anxiously. Rra is the last to greet me, which isn't unusual. She is like the runt in stature, but not personality – at least once you get to know her. Since we are surrounded, she goes for a simple tangle and keeps her jokes to herself.

Pa grabs my hand in his, leading me toward their dining room as Hoga takes a step beside me, giving a sharp sniff.

"You smell like the crystals, hø. Have you been praying for a *ĝha* again?" Hoga's narrowed eyes become pinpricks as the color of ice overtakes them.

"I have prayed for Wupeso, as I do with every rising of the sun," I say, stepping into their eating space. I have also prayed for my *ĝha*, but she does not need to know that. I cross my legs beneath me to sit near the table. They have fresh rainwater in a communal bowl and little pink slices of the Ugi fruit. Rra puts a pinch of *okkoran* dust over my serving before sliding it in front of me.

Birds squawk and trill outside as they flit among the trees, and a warm breeze pushes through the wide-open floors. It doesn't take them long to settle beside me, but with each seated *peholoe*, my nerves rise until it feels like a crackled sky across my *jisa*. Pa sits across from me and folds the end of his tail over his chest. He is nervous. The elders settle in around us and eat in silence. The sweet fruit juices bathe my tongue, and a hum of satisfaction works through me, even as I feel on the island's edge. Settling my half-finished slice of *ugi* fruit, I breathe away the cracks in my *jisa*.

"Rihu said you wanted to speak with me. Please, speak."

Pa nervously shifts his eye pigment from Hoga to me, hoping she will speak for him. I don't know what they did to convince Pa to be the spokesperson for their request, but I'm impressed when he finally speaks.

"We are worried for you." He starts. Nothing is new about this. They are always worried about me. They always ask me about my health and my home. They always drop in with fresh food and the details of their days. They always remind me to care for my body and mind. None of this is surprising. What he says next is.

"We think in light of the situation, it would be better for you to allow the *peholoe* to step in as tribal leaders. We have not discovered new lands; the women of the closest neighboring tribe were hit by some terrible disease. There is no way to right this catastrophic wrong, and we don't want you to lead a dying tribe."

The shock must crackle along my *jisa* once again because Rra shivers beside me. Hoga glares in my direction, but for once, she keeps her mouth shut as Pa speaks.

"You are a great Rogeshu, but when there is no village, there is nothing to lead," Pa tells me as if I did not already know. He does not know that I have made many considerations about how I can save our tribe. I considered sending Rihu and Royi past the crystal fields and across the seas. I negotiated with the neighboring tribe, but they did not have women to spare. I even asked Soekho The Remaining if she would consider a pleasure relationship, to which she promptly divided me of my *jisa*, divulging her great displeasure. I believe in Baso Sheva's rebirth, and she *will* save our tribe, but my belief may not be enough for many. That is what the *peholoe*'s words confirm.

"Baso Sheva will be reborn. It is cut in the crystals."

"We do not know Baso Sheva's time. Her rebirth could be in one moon or in one thousand."

I respect Pa for his wisdom, but my *jisa* shutters in panic, making me feel weak.

"*Peholoe*, please. Give me three moons to remedy our situation. If I cannot, then you can enact the Law of Wisdom and take my place to ease the loss of the tribe."

Jigu's face has fallen, and Gowi twines her tail in hers. My own faith in our rebirth has not been enough for the *peholoe*. They lose hope, even now. Strengthening my *jisa*, I sit taller. Hoga looks furious, but I press.

"Three moons. Keep the faith for three moons."

"You are foolish." Hoga snaps, draining the color from Jigu's eyes.

Pa rests his free hand over Hoga's and confirms, "Three moons and no more."

CHAPTER FIVE

The lights went dark inside the chamber, aside from the glowing blue entrances of the pod doors. The sounds of screaming in the corridors burned its way into my brain, and blood pounded in my ears. Aston tugs on my arm, but I can't feel it. Instead, my ears ring, and blackness starts to take the edges of my vision. Her green eyes swim before mine, and I try to blink back the panic. I wasn't one to have panic attacks. I was good at keeping my emotions close to the chest. But what started as a vacation to space has turned into a sci-fi horror film. I wanted to check out.

Aston taps the center of my chest, and I drag in a full breath. The blackness around the edges of my vision fades, and everything goes into hyperdrive. The alarms are different than before. Instead of a monotonous beep, beep, beep, it is a tinny screaming sound that never stops. Most of the men have evacuated, and I can hear the rending of flesh and their groans and screams beyond the sealed walls. The click of the speakers goes on, and my ears tune to the sounds.

A heavy breath, a groan, then a weak, "Escape if you can." The speakers click dead as the alarms go silent. The doorways on the far wall slide open, and the blood from the halls slide out across the tiled floors. The severed head of an aristocrat tumbled to the floor of the escape room with a thud, and one of the remaining children screamed. The narrow halls are bathed in red light, and bodies that have been destroyed are packed down as monsters walk over them.

An alien, the size of the entire foyer, is covered in green scales, with the upper body of a lizard man and the lower body of an armored spider. Chitinous legs stab through the mangled bodies of the dead as they crawl forward, filling the doorways.

"That's our cue." I choke, grabbing Aston's hand. I run as fast as I can into the nearest pod, looking at the panel with every intention of slamming the door closed. Glancing through the doorway, I watch the first monster enter the chamber. His claws rend the metallic partial wall like a knife through butter, and the cry of a child rings out. The half-dozen eyes dotted across the monster's mottled face are black and glassy, and the holes of his nose flatten as he sniffs the air. With preternatural ease, his eyes lock onto the small child from earlier as her mother steps between them. The woman shakes as she stares down the monster, and I curse under my breath.

"Hold the door," I tell Aston, physically placing her body in the frame.

Guards shuffle the survivors into the remaining pods, but when the aliens break through, the sound of gunfire explodes inside the chamber. Bullets fly toward the beasts, hit their armored skin, and drop to the ground dully. Still, it draws the predators' attention. Avoiding the line of fire, I run, never stopping as I scoop up the child and run back toward the pod where Aston leans against the doorframe.

"Run," I shout at the child's mother, looking back only momentarily. She doesn't hesitate to listen, turning away from the beast and following me back into the pod's safety. Falling to my knees in front of the control pad, I read the glowing little buttons as fast as humanly possible. Hitting the button that says close, I glance up to see a guard backing toward the door as her gun fires at the closest alien lifeform. She hits the beast in the eye, and he roars, pulling a clawed hand up to his face. His remaining eyes seek her out, and the door seals faster.

She glances back at the door, and her eyes widen. Then, firing off one more shot, she doesn't wait to see if it lands before running toward the door and slipping through just in time. She sighs, smiles, and taps a button on the panel. The door seals us in, and my stomach drops as the pod tumbles into space.

" Roxie Holt," the guard says, holding out her hand. It's so casual that my head spins. When I don't take her hand, she shrugs, tucking her gun back into her holster and patting her hands together to brush off the traces of gunpowder. Her eyes scan the room, and I watch, mesmerized, as her lips count the number of people in our pod.

There are a whopping eighteen of us with the girl and her mother – nearly double what the pod can support. I hear Aston's signature whimper, and my heart drops as I see her tears drip down her face. I watch the two teen boys walk across the pod, leaving the man beside them alone and sitting beside Aston. One rests an open palm on her knee and doesn't even flinch when Aston grabs onto it tight. The other sits with his brother, watching Aston sob and offering a packet of tissues from his pocket.

When Aston gives him a funny look and another pitiful sob, he shrugs. "Mom made us carry the things she couldn't. Pocket equality."

That makes Aston laugh, and I survey the rest of our pod-mates. Immediately to Aston's side, the woman and her curly-haired daughter sit together. The woman hums soothingly to her child, rocking them back and forth on the floor. Roxie is directly across from them, flashing a pocket light in the eyes of the only man aboard the escape pod. His jaw is set tight, and I can see the green of his eyes matches the twins. A brother, then.

Beside him, a little group of women is crowded around a stroller, rocking it back and forth. Peeking between the women, I see the rosy cheeks of a babe with bronzed skin. Rounded lips suckle the air.

Finally, at the back of the pod, two women who couldn't be more different sit with two kids. A dark-skin woman with a bright magenta frow and a pierced septum holds the hands of the older girl and spins the daisy on the girl's ring. They speak together in hushed tones, glancing at the woman with stick-straight blonde hair beside them. A little boy with matching platinum strands has his arms out wide as he tries to tell her about how big the aliens looked, and she nods nervously, trying to blink back tears while keeping the smile strapped to her face.

Roxie makes her way around the group, and when everyone seems in working order, she finds her way back to me. Roxie smiles at me and claps her hands on my shoulders.

"You're up." She says, flashing the light in my eyes without warning. She presses her fingers to the side of my neck and watches the hand of her watch spin, counting under her breath like she did moments ago. My vitals must be within acceptable ranges because she nods a moment later and goes back to play with the data pad.

In the fight, strands of Roxie's silky black hair fell out of her ballet bun, and she pushed it behind her ear, tapping away at the pad. A few moments later, a happy *beep, beep, boop* sounds, and the image of a blooming flower dissipates across the control panel, taking over the buttons.

A robotic feminine voice announces, "Thank you for enabling synthetic intelligence. My name is Blossom. You are aboard escape pod three of the *SS Herculean* with three days of support at current capacity. What are your names?"

"Commander Roxie Holt," Roxie begins, looking at me.

"Vera Oksana," I say, turning my eyes toward Aston.

"Aston Andrews," she murmurs. The boys follow her lead, and I learn they are Cain and Abel. The older guy across the ship is their brother Zachary. As Blossom goes around cataloging the names, I realize that there are quite a few siblings on the pod. When Blossom is finished, she addresses the group.

"Nice to meet you, occupants of *SS Herculean EP3*. How may I help you today?"

Roxie doesn't give any of the panicking people behind me a chance to speak as she jumps headfirst into her questions. "What are your capabilities?"

"I have many capabilities. Would you like me to list my most common uses?"

"Yes." Roxie half-shouts.

"I can tell you about your distance from the SS Herculean, earth, and potentially habitable planets. I can adjust pod settings like lighting, sound, and various modes. I can seek refuge, and I can —"

"That one. Seek refuge." Roxie interrupts.

"Processing." Blossom hums and elevator music plays as she processes Roxie's request.

The girl with the icy blonde hair practically shouts, "What does seek refuge even do?"

"And how far are we from Earth?" the goth girl beside her asks.

"Are we going home?" the curly-haired daughter adds.

Her mother whispers, "I don't know, sweetie."

Blossom interrupts the outbreak of whispers with, "You are one day and fifteen hours from refuge. According to the biological data I've gathered, I would recommend entering sleep mode. Would you like me to set the pod to sleep mode?"

Roxie glances around the room, and everyone nods voraciously. "Yes. Set pod to sleep mode."

Blossom directs us on where to stand as the pod transforms before our eyes. Walls slide open, revealing single beds with luxury sheets, and the scent of lavender overtakes the space. Meal bars in silver packaging sit beside a clear-wrapped chocolate chip cookie and a tiny water bottle. Everyone claims their bunks, and soft white noise plays quietly as we settle. I get into my bed and lean against the back of the bunk while I eat my meal bar. When Aston grabs hers, I pat the space beside me. She doesn't hesitate to climb in, and her chilly fingers latch onto mine.

"At least there's chocolate." She says, lifting the cookie.

I roll my eyes, "Yes, at least there's chocolate."

It doesn't take long for her to drift off to sleep. The kids are all snoring by the hour's end. Still, as I look around, I don't think I'm the only person who didn't sleep a wink.

CHAPTER SIX

When I close my eyes, my mind concocts images of red lighting and evil monsters. So, instead, I focus on the soft breaths of Aston beside me. Her arm is slung over my belly, and her face is relaxed. I'm grateful she can sleep, even if I'm jealous. I ground myself with an old technique Ralph taught me during one of his smoke breaks. Five things I can see – the glow of Blossom's data pad, a cookie wrapper at the foot of the bed, Aston's chest rising and falling, the metallic floor beside me, Roxie sneaking across the pod. *Wait.*

Carefully, I remove Aston's arm from my body, replacing myself with a spare pillow. Tip-toeing across the room, I beg the rubber soles of my chucks to be silent on the shiny floors. My attempt at stealth doesn't work, and Roxie whirls around, her gun drawn. Seeing it's only me, she again tucks the gun into her holster.

"Jesus," She whispers, "Warn a girl, won't you?" Roxie turns the volume down on Blossom and taps through a few data pages. I crowd behind her to watch before a silent image of what happened on the SS Herculean appears. First, there are images of the asteroid belt we hit. Next, we see how the ship ran headfirst into one rock, then another, and a third before stabilization. All the emergency response protocols had worked, so we could see the emergency walls shutter into place. Then, the healed but incomplete version of the ship starts navigating through the remainder of the asteroid belt. But the asteroid belt wasn't done with us; apparently, these rocks were home to something. The rocks converge on the most broken end of the ship.

Like stepping on an ant hill, the terrifying creatures we encountered crawl out of the space rocks, cutting through the metal of the *SS Herculean* like they did the hallways and moving through the ship. Roxie pushes to different camera angles, and I watch in horror as they work their way into the tunnels, cutting down people left and right. They seem to speak to one another as they move systematically and intelligently. The beasts clear corridor after corridor, room after room. Roxie pulls the videos from the captain's helm, the evacuation room, and the tunnels, and they all play simultaneously in all their horrific detail. I watch the captain and his guards fire at the beasts until their guns run out of bullets. Then, I watch the monsters rend the guards to pieces as the captain speaks his final message, "Escape if you can."

One of the monster's chitinous legs stabs through the captain's chest, and I flinch. Bile rises to the back of my throat. I look away.

When I've gained control of my stomach, I look back, but red lights flash, and blocky letters reveal, "Corrupted File." Roxie tries to fix it, pulling up a command prompt and typing like mad, but the synthetic intelligence takes over. It immediately blocks the corrupted file and our connection to the *SS Herculean*. Her words, though quiet, still ring out through the space.

"Connection to *SS Herculean* severed."

"Well, shit," Roxie huffs, pulling the data pad to the floor with her. I flinch at her language. After years of being cussed at by my family, then boyfriends, then men in crappy places, I always expected words like that to come with a beating. But I wasn't on Earth, and somehow, I survived the slaughter I had just watched. So, I doubted my dysfunction mattered much anymore.

"Do you think we hurt those creatures' homes? Do you think they were just trying to protect themselves?" I ask, a shiver working its way over my body at the pure flood of scaled bodies and armored legs I had seen. The moment the words left my mouth, they felt silly – like toxic positivity as a cure for depression, a slaughter of that extent wasn't an answer to an accident.

"The ship took most of the damage, and those monsters were intelligent," Roxie explains, shaking her head.

"Do you think they knew we were coming? Like they had a web ready to catch us in?"

Roxie studies hyperdrive data I have zero understanding of, tabbing through file after file to find some kind of answer. Her frustration gains the best of her, and she closes every open window before powering off the data pad screen.

"I don't know, Vera. All I know is that their attack didn't seem provoked. It was too well-organized. They were too intelligent." Her eyes close, and I watch her hand stiffen above her weapon. She must be replaying what she can remember of the event, but when her eyes open again, she just shakes her head. "I'm concerned they'll follow the pods."

"Do you think they will follow us to the refuge planet?"

"We can hope not," Roxie replies. "Blossom, can you tell us if they are tracking the pod?"

"There are no life forms detected within threatened range." She replies in a soothing but robotic voice.

Roxie nods, her jaw tight, and I can tell she's not happy with Blossom's words. Just because we're not threatened right now doesn't mean we are safe. It doesn't mean whatever happened on the ship is over for good. I reach for her hand, and Roxie lets me hold it. Giving it a squeeze, I try to be encouraging.

"We'll make it to the refuge planet. We'll be safe there. I will make sure of it."

Roxie pulls her hand from mine and sucks in a breath. Her shoulders slump when she says, "You can't promise that."

CHAPTER SEVEN

Tonight, the moon will be whole once again, and tomorrow I will have to enact the Law of Wisdom and step aside for the *peholoe*'s guidance. Since our meeting, they have not bothered me or mentioned their lack of faith. I sent Rihu and Royi to explore an entire span of daylight in every direction, and they have found nothing but an endless sea and the village of our neighboring tribe. Unfortunately, the neighboring town still refuses to allow our men visitation to see if they find their *ĝha*. This is why I pray.

I knelt for so long that the ash of the crystals burrowed into my knees through my trousers. Still, I repeat plea after plea to the Baso Sheva. I am not so fearful of the *peholoe* ruling as what it will do to my people. By enacting the Law of Wisdom, I must admit that the tribe is dying, and I still hold faith it is not. I believe in my people and think we can find a way.

This rising, I sent Rihu to the neighboring village one last time and Royi in the final direction of the sun's spears. Unless they return with good news, I cannot find a solution without Baso Sheva's help. This is what I told her today. I explain to her all the lengths I have taken and all the faith I place in her. Being the Rogeshu is a privilege, and I am grateful for it, but there is little in my power that I can do now.

When the sun is high overhead, I am struck with the need to check on my fishers. I thank Baso Sheva and head back through the village.

Wupeso is a long, skinny island of the sea. I pray at the northwesternmost point in the crystal fields – the holy lands of Baso Sheva, where we can all recharge our *jisa*. I slowly work through the village, waving to the homes atop the karsts, watching the Zrew flap away from the treetops. I skirt the rocky cliffs to find Llazho sitting atop a rock at the entry to the bay. His nets are set in the shallows, two lines are set further in the deep, and he casts his own line into the water. The *unane* shell bobs on the surface. A woven basket sits in a shady area to the left, already filled with fish.

"Any luck?" I call from the ground, shading my eyes from the sun's light. I know Llazho doesn't like to be disturbed when he is fishing, but the Baso Sheva practically led me to him. *For what purpose?*

"Yes." Llazho is not a man of many words.

"May I fish with you?" I asked, climbing the rock he sat upon. He stares at me as if I've grown a third horn. It is true. I have had no interest in fishing with him since childhood. When I was younger, Llazho told me fishing was a quiet job. When I learned fishing was not necessarily a quiet job, Llazho was actually a quiet male, and it was determined I was a better fit for the skies. His eye color eclipses his sight momentarily, and he grunts in response, pointing at an extra line.

I sit beside him on the rock and cast my line in the opposite direction of his. It is quiet besides the lap of the waves and the sound of our breaths. The warmth of the sun glances off the water, making it glitter, and my soul feels at peace for a moment.

Llazho grunts beside me, and I watch his *unane* shell dip beneath the water momentarily before he pulls on his line. I want to jump and cheer for the moment of excitement, but I stay silent because I know the battle is not over yet. Llazho pulls his line, looping it around his forearm and then repeating the process. I can see the massive fish beneath the water as a cacophony of birds squawk above me. Tearing my eyes from the incredible catch, I search the skies.

Immediately, I am alarmed. Llazho pulls his fish to the shore behind me, and I hear him curse under his breath. It is proof I am not alone in what I see. It looks as if the moon is falling from the sky. A gigantic, shining silver ball plummets toward the sea so fast flame gathers along its face.

The color leeches from our eyes as we watch the ball grow larger as it gets closer. Grabbing Llazho by the arm, I pull him away from the beach, preparing for an overwhelming splash. Rihu and Royi run toward me, shouting something unintelligible. Before any more action can be taken, the hunk of metal plunges into the sea, splashing water in every direction for an entire *lushi*. The water cascades over us, reaching even the bottoms of the floating islands and bathing them in the salty splash.

The displaced seas wash the land on the way back to their homes, and the silver sphere pops to the surface like a massive *unane* shell, bobbing on the waves. The sun hits it exactly right, and the sharp light in my eyes makes my color overtake them. My *jisa* crackles to life a moment too late, and I look around at the males. We look ridiculous. We are all dripping, and my ordinarily airy white shirt suctions to my skin uncomfortably. Royi's typically light hair is sopping and dark. Llazho looks ready to join the warriors, especially as he strips off his shirt, growling as it gets caught on a horn.

Rihu points towards the bay, and I watch as the waves push the massive ball against the entrance to the bay. The water of the floating falls crashes against the side before trailing back to the water below. Many of the males and children have gathered around the shining ball, and one of the Vukusugo stabs at it with their sword. I hop from the rock and groan at the mess of Llazho's gear before heading in the direction of the ball.

Rihu and Royi stand behind me with the Vukusugo behind them. Then, without a sound, a hole opens in the ball, and Baso Sheva answers my prayers.

CHAPTER EIGHT

Vera

So, that sucked. Crash-landing on a ninety-six percent habitable planet is an experience I never wanted – on this trip or ever again. Worse, thirty-six hours is not nearly enough time to come to terms with the fact that you're not landing on Earth or being saved by a new ship. It's not enough time to process that you're about to land on a completely unexplored planet. And it is definitely not enough time to prepare for what the doors open up to.

Aston screams at the new aliens, sliding behind me and Roxie, who has her gun pulled in seconds. Blossom, who put us here for refuge, announces, "Congratulations! Occupants of *SS Herculean EP3*, you have made first contact."

My eyes scan the aliens and the land carefully. What looks like rows of crops in various shades of green, blue, and orange are surrounded by fences and well-tended behind the dozens of curious aliens. Unlike the monsters we encountered on the ship, these look almost human. They also look entirely masculine. Muscled, tall, and deadly, some stand with swords drawn while others ripple with tension. I can't find a feminine one among them, but maybe that is how they look.

At the front of the group, a remarkably handsome alien draws my attention. Their eyes are different than ours; they have dark pupils, and the rims of their eyes are ringed in color. Except with his, the color seems to overtake him, bringing the pupil to a pinpoint and exposing the brightest jade color I've ever seen. His skin is so dark a green that it would seem almost black without the silver markings lightening the skin around them. His eyes meet mine, and a single alien word escapes.

"Adjay." He smiles widely, looking back at his people as he babbles. Blossom immediately tunes in to the chatter.

Her feminine, robotic voice says, "Processing language."

Roxie is still at a standstill beside me; her finger is still stacked behind the trigger. The women cower behind us, and the aliens seem surprised by whatever the man has said. They look at us with new interest, making us even more nervous. The aliens stop speaking to one another as Blossom speaks again.

"These are the V`òllø people. They speak V`òlløaian. Based on my gathered intelligence, they are generally kind to females and usually non-hostile to outsiders. For best refuge integration, I recommend placing me in full-body mode."

Roxie immediately caves to her wish, "Blossom, please enter full-body mode. And translate."

The man who turned away with his smile puts his eyes back on me, and a shiver works its way through my body. It's like a mirage shimmers over his body, and I watch a crackle of silver seemingly spark off of him.

"Yu gah chew ho-she?" He asks slowly, keeping his intense gaze on mine. I look at the ship and ask Blossom to translate. She tells me that he wants to know my name. Or what he can call me.

"Vera," I say, giving Roxie side-eye. Aston's hands come around my arms, and her nails dig into me a little too hard. I wince, and his eye color immediately dims; his mouth turns down in the seemingly universal sign of displeasure.

"Oh grr-o tu." He practically shouts, eyes flicking between Aston and myself. "A Vera."

The way he says my name makes me oddly pleased. Meanwhile, Aston whimpers behind me, her nails tightening into my arm further. The alien's eyes widen as a drop of blood oozes down my arm, and he lunges forward before the man beside him grabs his shoulder, wrenching him back.

I turn away from him and slowly peel Aston's hands from my arm, urging her to look at what she's done. She got me back there, in the tunnels of the ship, and I had to tell her repeatedly that I wasn't upset with her, even as the alcohol wipes on the escape pod burned. I brought her on this trip and take full responsibility for her terror, even if she takes it out on my body. But, as far as Blossom can tell, we are safe here. This planet was our best option, and that includes its people.

"Sorry," She whimpers, flicking her eyes between me and the alien that lunged for her.

The crowd of aliens seems to turn as more approach, and I can see Roxie tense further. There are not many aliens, but she is one girl with one gun. We asked if the escape pod had any defenses and were met with an answer akin to, 'What for?' One Roxie vs. what looks like about fifty aliens was not an odd I would bet on, even though I believe she is an incredible fighter. Many of the males step back for the new arrivals and take their place one step behind the male, who won't stop looking at me.

Blossom translates one of the new arrivals, "She is your soulmate?"

His head tilts to the right, and Blossom translates his following words, "Do you not hear her heart?"

"Yes, but I would see yours." Blossom translates, but I listen to the alien's voice. It is more feminine, even as the tone is commanding. She is dressed in a long linen dress and sandals, and her hair looks silkier. Her horns curl at the ends differently. I believe she is the first female alien I've seen. My head tilts to the side, and I look at her skin. It seems more crystalline in texture, and she has significantly more marks than the male she speaks to.

My eyes flick between them, and he strips away his shirt, which I only now notice was so wet it was sticking to his frame. Two matching silver marks sit above both pecs on a flat chest with no nipples. It's like two diamonds with a line through it and a droplet at the bottom drawn in the same silver color as the swirls over his shoulders and arms. Another female alien sees them and gasps. Blossom translates.

"A soulmate!"

I'm about to turn to the ship to ask what's going on when a beautiful rose-gold robot steps forward. Her eyes glow lilac, and she would look like one of us if our skin was made of metal and we dressed in scant armor. Her joints are silent as she steps to the front of the group and introduces herself in the alien's language, simultaneously projecting the translation to us.

"I am Blossom. Thank you for welcoming us to your world. I can tell the women of any words you speak."

From there, she passes us each an earpiece, telling us she can process multiple inputs simultaneously. With the earpiece, as long as she is within hearing range, she can translate individual conversations to the prescribed individuals. We all put the pieces in as Blossom addresses the aliens once again.

"May we step onto your lands?"

One of the females says, "Yes, please. Welcome, - I do not know what to call you."

"I am Blossom, a synthetic intelligence. These are humans, and their names are," Blossom rattles them off as her robotic digits point at each of us. "What are your names?"

The male at the front, who is clearly the leader says, "Kano."

It's so masculine, just like him, and I want to repeat it, but he's staring so intently at my mouth that I keep it closed.

Behind him, a man introduces himself as Ree-Who and then winks at Aston, who buries her face in my back like a child. Still, I let her cling to me like the other children cling to their siblings and Alba. When many of the introductions are made, Kano tells his people to disperse and prepare a welcome feast. Then, he and a group he calls the *Peholoe*, which Blossom translates as elders without souls – ominous, make space for us to step out of the ship. Roxie puts her gun away and scans the area.

To me, it looks a lot like Earth. The plants are different colors, but plenty of greens and browns still exist. The water is still blue, though the sky looks more purple. Birds, bigger than any I have ever seen, fly overhead and squawk in a terribly normal tone. But then, there are things that are not like Earth. The dirt is bluish-gray, and the crops can't be described as anything but alien. Large portions of the land are covered in shade, and when I look up, I see why. Chunks of land float high above us in indescribable glory. A waterfall crashes down from one of the floating islands and tumbles against the unnaturally smooth curve of the escape pod.

I'm pulled out of my reverie when one of the women says, "The humans can stay in the *peholoe* loft. It is big enough for them all."

Kano's tail slashes across the air in front of his chest, and he says, "No, they will stay among the people on the ground."

"That is ridiculous." The woman huffs. "Let them stay in the loft. Do you not want the best for your soulmate?"

The only male in the *peholoe* calls the female Hoga when he tells her to leave it. Kano sighs in annoyance, turning to me. I take Aston's hand in mine, and she gives it a comforting squeeze as we are brought to a stop. He seems to glare at her hand in mine, but I tilt my face up to his, nonetheless.

38

In my ear, I hear, "What would you prefer, my Vera?"

I lick my lips, and the center-point of his eyes track the movement of my tongue. I glance back at the group of women and say, "Maybe we can see both and then make a decision?"

Kano smiles brightly, and I feel as if I've pleased him. That sends the butterflies diving in my stomach, and a blush rises to my cheeks. I've never been so easily manipulated by a human man, but this alien seems to see right through me. I don't know that I could lie to him if I tried.

Onward our tour goes, first showing us the tribal meeting hut and a large barracks area. They both seem somewhat human – shelters built above ground with beds and seating made of wood and plant fibers. We are extra careful when we navigate the bridge over a wide chasm. Blossom explains that it is mostly safe during the day, but everyone should still be careful because the chasm has monsters of its own. One of the twins asks about the colorful blue mushrooms, and Blossom is the one to tell us that they may have adverse effects on humans. We've only seen half the island by the time the sun starts setting, and Alba is exhausted from carrying the baby and keeping Caroline's hand in hers. In fact, all the kids are grouchy as the sky turns from lilac to violet.

Roxie grunts unhappily beside me, but she doesn't voice any of her concerns with the group. In fact, since we stepped on this planet, it seems like she's taken a backseat – only wanting to lead where she is comfortable.

As I look around our group, I realize how tired we all really are. I know I didn't sleep on the ship, no matter how much white noise Blossom played. And I can see the toll this unwanted adventure takes on our group. The children grow fussy, cry, and snap at their designated adults. The twins want to touch everything we pass, and Zach has their tiny hands in his fists. When I first saw Alba, I thought she was beautiful, but now she looks bedraggled and exhausted. Worst yet, Aston has wholly lost her sparkle. Someone has to do something, and since it won't be Blossom – due to her having no idea of the toll, and it won't be Roxie, it will have to be me.

"Kano," I say, stopping the group and placing a hand on his arm. His eyes seem to light up as he spins to face me. That heart-melting smile has my heart galloping in my chest. I pull my hand away from his skin and take a step back. "Is there somewhere the children and women can rest? You can show me, and any of the other adults who would like to continue the tour, where the loft is. Everyone is quite tired after our journey."

His brows are furrowed, and he looks at me with the same intent as before. It seems to say, 'Anything for you, Vera.' I look away back toward the women and children, and he nods.

"Of course, my Vera. The *peholoe* can show them to the tribal hut again. Pa can carry the nursling. That is where the welcome meal will be in two suns."

I realize Blossom didn't translate that to everyone, so I let the women and children know the plan. Aston, though she is exhausted, wants to stay with me. And surprisingly, a woman named Cerridwen invites herself along. She looks the least tired of the bunch, which is weird. But weirder is that she actually looks a bit excited. Blossom stays with us, determining that they can safely make it to the hut without any communication issues.

"To the floating islands now?" Cerridwen asks. If Kano is surprised by her excitement, he doesn't show it. He tilts his head to the right and keeps walking. Blossom is the one who tells us that a right head tilt seems to be like a human nod.

As we walk through the village, we have to go back over the chasm – terrifying, through the farmlands we landed by –

40

colorful, and along the edge of a mountain across a beautiful black-sand beach. The water is still unsettled, and our escape pod looks wrong against the horizon. The silver ball is so unnatural that even as the water cascades along it, splashing into the bay, it looks out of place. Kano doesn't seem to mind, though. He looks at it in awe, pressing a clasped fist against his forehead and thanking the Baso Sheva – whatever that is.

Finally, we reach the bottom of the karst with steps carved into the sides like a spiral staircase. I've never been afraid of heights, but Aston is. That means she clings to the inside karst wall and has a hand gripping the rope railing like the stairs will drop out under her at any minute. I feel a little bad, but I'm grateful she doesn't grab onto my arm that way again. Aston is terrified, and I feel like it's ultimately my fault. I won the tickets, I invited her on the trip, I told her it would be safe and fun. Now, she's stuck on a habitable planet that is apparently full of aliens in the same dirty clothes from days ago. I would cry, too, if I wasn't too busy feeling loads of guilt.

The steps are exhausting, and I pant for breath by the time we reach the top. The air up here is clearly thinner, but the sun's warmth and the trees' density take my breath away. Trees of green and pink are packed so tightly together that it acts as a roof to the forest floor. Well-worn walking trails are evident against the underbrush as the same bluish-gray dirt is dark with the humidity. Kano doesn't hesitate to lead us through the trails.

A beautiful tree house is built into the canopy not too far from the landing. Kano leads us up a graded platform and into the jungle home; it's wide open and expansive. Well-made wooden shutters are opened, and a cross-breeze brushes through, drying the sweat on my neck. If we were on earth, seeing this place, I would expect it to be a million-dollar tree home from some kind of Netflix special, but here on this planet, it was the home of the *peholoe*. Notable in its own right, but not a million-dollar resort where the waterspouts drop from the wall with the press of a button.

Cerridwen, Aston, and I spread out slightly, walking through the space within eyesight of one another. At the far back, a wall of stone has been built, and water drips down it into a stone bowl below. A large, smoothed stump sits off to one side of the space, with another bowl of food placed at its center. Woven mats surround a pile of bark chips, and I gravitate toward them. Kneeling on the mat, I look at the chips.

Little runes are carved into the faces of each chip. In the whole stack, there are only two I recognize. They match the tattoos on Kano's still-bare chest. Blossom scans the area and processes a map of the island. Cerridwen stands outside the slatted doors, breathing in the fresh island air. Aston has even left her fear for awe as she explores the bedrooms. I'm looking at the chips trying to figure out what they use them for when Aston comes out half-shouting.

"I found a bathroom! There's a hot spring. And a toilet that's not a bucket."

Cerridwen and I immediately rush to her side, following her into the wide-open room. It's more like a bathhouse. The hot spring is a wide rectangular pool, and steam rises up onto the walls. The wood seems to seek moisture, but there isn't a smell of mildew, but rather a scent akin to eucalyptus or mint. She pushes her way through the chamber and shows us three little stalls at the back. Sure enough, a tiny room reminiscent of a portable bathroom is there, filled with the sound of rushing water.

When we come out of the bathroom, Kano sits cross-legged by the stump, bringing a slice of pink fruit to his lips. The color in his face blanches when he sees us, and I can't help but smile. He looks like a kid caught with his hand in the cookie jar.

"It's my favorite." He says as a way of explanation. Cerridwen and Aston's good mood fades at the sight of him, but mine doesn't. I pad across the room and sit beside him, holding out an open palm for a piece. My stomach grumbles when the hint of spice wrinkles my nose. He places it in my hand, and I give Blossom a curious look.

"It's safe?"

Blossom replies, "Yes, the fruit of the *diodia amulea* appears safe for human consumption."

I take a bite, and my tongue is thoroughly confused. The fruit tastes delicious, but unlike anything I've ever had before. It's the texture of an orange, dusted in something like spicy sugar. It's sweet and spicy and salty and fresh. It would be like sweet chili oil over cake batter if it had the pulpy texture of an orange. I'm not sure how to describe it. Then, turning toward Aston, I offer her the other bite of my slice.

"You have to try this."

Her lips turn down, and her nose wrinkles unattractively. She leans away from my outstretched hand. "I'm not sure I want to."

I roll my eyes, popping the piece in my mouth and putting my palm out for another. This makes Kano very happy, and he sprinkles a bit of the salt stuff over the fruit before handing me another slice. We finish our fruit while Cerridwen and Aston ask Blossom questions about the tree house and island. Between bites, I ask Kano about the village.

Blossom's translations enter my ear at the same time as his language, and I focus hard on his words to try and learn. "The village is Wupeso. We are not many. Our neighbors are more. I am the village leader. You lead the soulmates?"

"Adjay?" I repeat, trying to understand. Blossom translates it as soulmate, but I feel like that can't be right.

"Women." He says, using a different word than before. It makes me think of Roxie and Blossom, and I'm not sure I would call myself their leader. I think I work best under pressure. So, instead of answering, I take the opportunity to chew politely and think about how to answer his question. I look at Aston and Cerridwen and see their exhaustion weighing on them. If I'm their leader, I'm not doing a great job.

"We are a team." I finally say, swallowing my bite.

I don't want our conversation to be over when the fruit is gone. Kano is nice. He's easy to talk to. But this tiny fruit date was like a commercial break from reality. My team and I were still stranded on this alien planet. Half of them were on the ground, probably asleep on some dusty foreign floor or trying to feed the baby the ship's supply of formula. While the four of us were here, I was selfishly gorging myself on fruit that I decided tasted like spicy cake batter.

I stand from the floor and dust off my jeans, cringing at the grime and blood staining the wide hems. The commercial break was nice, but we should really catch back up with the other humans.

"I think the women will like it here. It has a bathroom like on Earth and a sense of privacy." I announce, bringing a slight frown to Kano's lips. Still, he nods in agreement and escorts us back down the karst to be reunited with the other women.

CHAPTER NINE

I still can't sleep the first night in the loft. Aston and I volunteered to share a room so Alba could have one of her own instead of sharing it with Caroline and the baby. It wasn't like we weren't best friends with an extensive background of successful sleepovers, right? So, why were her light sleepy breaths grating my nerves? Why did my skin feel like it was itching? Why, even though I was conceptually safe, couldn't I sleep to the jungle-themed white noise like I did at home?

I try to close my eyes, but glowing emerald eyes fill my vision immediately, dragging me back to the moment we stepped onto this planet. It felt so chaotic, and everyone froze behind me, but there was this light in the darkness. Some weird alien eyes that seemed to calm me. It's why I was able to respond, and that didn't make any sense. I should have been equally fearful and frozen as the rest.

As my eyes rest, I can hear his voice, but in English. Calling me his soulmate and thanking a higher power for delivering me to him. I feel his massive hands wrap around me, and it makes me think of an awful time on Earth. Instead of the comforting alien's grip, its panic made human.

My eyes snap open. I'm met with shadows and moonlight cutting its way through the loft's trees and open walls. The ceiling above me is a weave of living branches through slats of board expertly locked together. Beyond that, I hear Aston's deep, sleepy breath, and I can't help but groan. It's never bothered me before, but right now, it's like nails on a chalkboard.

Stepping out of bed, I pad out to the main living area. A small glowing crystal is set at the center of the stump table, releasing an emanating light. I scan the room for a place to post up and think, but a dark figure sits in the corner. A light gasp escapes me at the alien woman contentedly sitting in the darkness. Her horned head curves toward mine, and she tilts her horns to the right.

"Sorry. Can't sleep," I whisper, knowing the woman won't understand. I tip-toed my way across the room, finding a seat on the mat across from her and watching her arrange little runic wood chips in different patterns. She seems so focused as she moves more rounded fragments into a circle off to the side while shuffling the rest of the chips back and forth. As she moves around the pieces, I inspect her face. She's familiar from our arrival but so alien to look at. Her skin is a light shade of blue with a subtle silver sheen that catches and reflects the moonlight. Her long, sinuous tail flicks restlessly behind her as she plays with her chips.

"Hoga?" I ask, hoping that my inflection will translate easily.

"Jè," she replies, tilting her head to the right again, forcing her simple steel-colored braid to tap her shoulder. Her eyes, a similar color to her hair, narrow on me.

Unsure if that's a yes or a no, I place a palm to my chest and say, "I'm Vera."

Hoga gives me a blank look before repeating, "Jè," and tilting her head. It seems jè does, in fact, mean yes. Then, she pulls two matching chips from her pile and points at them with her long, intricately tattooed fingers.

"Kano, oh Vera." She says, sliding the chips next to one another. "Adjay. Jè."

I have no clue what she's saying other than Kano's name and my own, but I nod my head along, repeating, "Jè. Jè. Kano, jè."

Hoga smirks and a shiver works its way down my spine. My instincts seem to catch up with me as I realize I know very little about this V`òllø woman. But the way she looks at me when I agree with her about knowing Kano brings me much-needed clarification. I would know this kind of woman on any planet. Hoga was not the sweet old lady who offered to share her home as I once suspected. No, she was the cutthroat woman who had experienced loss and grief. Hoga had a stake in the game and lost. And that loss made her the woman she was today. A woman who couldn't sleep peacefully and wouldn't be refused. Still, I try.

"Maybe I should get Blossom?" I offer, moving to stand, hoping to escape. But Hoga won't have it. Instead, she grabs my hand and tugs me back to the mat. Then, she shuffles the chips by stirring them in a pile. They all roll back so the runes point upward. That is when she stops.

She organizes the chips into the three lines between us, then pulls a chip from the center line and places it off to the side. She pauses and looks at me. I pick a matching chip and place it off to the side, mirroring her. She tilts her head to the right with a predatory smile, and I offer her a half-grimace. She moves another chip, and I try to follow her lead. She tilts her head to the right when I've done something correctly and to the left if I try to make some kind of illegal move. Then, she hisses, "G'u'. G'u'," when I try to take one of the Kano chips while the other one is still in a line. At some point, she uses a chip with a little swirly rune on it to take a chip from my circle and complete her own. Hoga is very pleased by that move.

I watch her pick up the Kano chip, and I go to shout, "G'u'" at her, but then she uses a chip with two circles at the bottom of an open triangle to pick up the other one. Hoga smiles at me like she's won, and I know she has. Not that I learned how to play before now.

She points at the two Kano cards and says, "Kano o Vera, Adjay. D'o go chu merchu, Baso Sheva."

"Yeah, yeah," I grumble, disappointed with my loss. "You won, you old bat."

She begins shuffling the chips once again, and I sigh, looking out the window. I learned a lot from this first round about how the game is played, but it's still complicated and alien. It reminds me of poker but requires a lot more luck. It seemed like all the stars had to align for me to win this game, whereas poker was more about bluffing my way through. While Hoga shuffles, I look at the moon-bathed jungle outside. It's like an earth forest, except different. Some leaves look red and dewy in the moonlight, like blood on the pavement. The undergrowth looms higher than that on Earth, reaching up the tree trunks like tentacles. Even the sounds are alien. Aside from the usual trickling of water, the noises are quiet and eerie. A soft, shuttling hiss stutters and stops before going again. Gruff groans echo through, and horrifying caws flutter among the leaves. Instead of that purely earthen smell, like the air after rain, the one here is a touch saltier and more heated, similar to the scent of aloe baked onto your skin by the summer sun.

Hoga calls my name, and I snap out of my reverie, returning to our game. This next round, I'm better prepared for. Or at least, I think I am until about four moves into the game; Hoga grabs a rune that looks like the triple goddess symbol and uses it to unbury both Kano runes. She sits in front of me like she's won once again, and I know she has.

Frustration laces through me as I dedicate my focus to learning this game. We played three more times before I truly had the hang of it. Then, as the sunrise starts, I finally win. My circle is built, I have an equal number of swirly chips and upside-down V-chips, and the Kano chips are unburied. She finishes her circle and looks at me for my turn. I pull both

Kano chips off the three stacks and put them at the bottom of my similar lines. I look at her with a smirk, and she gives me a genuine smile for the first time tonight.

My excitement is palpable as I jump from the mat, grunting, "Yes! Finally!"

The same rush of a high-stakes poker game rushes through my veins, but then Hoga chuckles. My body stills, mid-fist-bump. Her icy blue brows narrow in my direction, and she pulls the freaking triple goddess chip from the center of her circle and steals the Kano chips from me. My smile drops.

"What?" I screech, kneeling on the mat, inspecting her chips. She completed her circle, which both protects and activates the triple goddess chip, but I didn't know you could use it after I had already seized the Kano chips. Blossom beeps to life at my noise, and the baby starts crying from the other room. Hoga laughs, standing from our game and toddling off to retrieve the crying child. When she returns, I'm still staring at the chips trying to figure out how she did that; how I didn't notice she had the trump card on her side.

My shout of disbelief must have scared Aston, too, because she comes stumbling out of our room dressed in nothing but her lacy underthings. She rubs her eyes to focus on the room spinning before her. Then, she sees me bent over the chips. All her sleepiness vanishes as she glares in my direction, hands fisted on her flared hips. She knows exactly what it looks like when I lose a gamble, and she doesn't like it one bit.

"We've been on an alien planet for less than a full day, and you're already gambling?" she asks, though her tone is reprimanding.

"I couldn't sleep," I shrug, hoarding my apologetic eyes for Hoga when I kick her butt in the next game. Aston huffs in annoyance before spinning on her toes and going back to bed. I hear the beads of the doorway clatter together and catch a final glimpse of her rear, shouting, "Rest well, sleeping booty."

Aston's middle finger pops out of the beaded entry before disappearing once again. This makes me laugh for the first time in days.

I shuffle the chips in the same manner I've seen Hoga do and plan out a few strategies in my head. A few of the women get moving for the day, and the other elders help them get dressed in some alien garb. Fuchsia linen dresses with dusty rose aprons, wide linen pants the same color as the dirt, and sleeveless cream tunics seem to be the options. While I shuffle and organize the game board, Hoga gets the baby back to happiness, feeding it some milk-like substance and changing its diaper for a cloth one. Then, as I'm about to call the V`òllø woman over, the deep voice that kept me from my dreams greets us from the doorway.

Blossom translates, "My Soul. My Vera."

CHAPTER TEN

My *ĝha* is even more beautiful than I remember. The view of My Vera's smile, bent over a game of *roshev*, has my hearts pounding double-time in my chest. I send up a prayer of thanks as I carry in the bundle of food I've brought for the humans. I want to drop the food where I stand and sweep my *ĝha* into my arms, but I resist. Bringing the food to the table, I untied the corners of the pouch and let the food tumble out into their organized pots and dishes.

My people sent this food as a gift. They wanted to deliver it themselves, but Pa pointed out that the humans may need time to acclimate. Still, my people are excited by the humans' arrival, and their faith in Baso Sheva has been restored. They wanted the women to feel welcome, and they were sure to tell me at the sun's first light. I had a line of men outside my door with goods for the women. Even the grouchy Llazho came with fish in hand.

It takes a few minutes to get everything in presentable order, and I expect to see my *ĝha* standing behind me when I finish. I turn to find that my woman has disappeared from the main room, and the tap of a beaded doorway still rings out. The other women approach the food cautiously, looking at the feast before them.

"It is all the very best foods," I promise, tilting my horns to Blossom in thanks for her translation. One woman with silky black hair is the first to try, picking up a slice of the *lore*-spiced fish with *shegi*-cooked flatbread. When she hums in delight, the other women descend, tentatively picking at the food before them. Watching them try the gifts of my people warmed my hearts, and I wished my *ĝha* would bring me this joy. But, instead, she hides from me. I can feel her presence beyond me, and I feel her rejection like an ice-crystal in my chest.

Standing from the table, the woman closest to me shifts away with a whimper. My brows pinch in confusion, but I lower my horns in her direction politely before stepping out. I'm two steps from the entry of my *ĝha*'s room when Hoga steps into my path. She is as off-putting as usual. This is only heightened by the fact that the humans trusted her with a nursling. The squishy human babe is fast asleep in the *g`ì*'s arms, unaware of the critical *peholoe* who holds her.

"They should not allow you near such small children." I joke, inspecting the scrunched face. The nursling could fit in one of my hands and still requires help supporting its own head. I've never seen Hoga be so gentle. It's too bad that nurturing doesn't extend to me.

"Do not bother her. She will come out when she is ready." Hoga demands, rocking the nursling gently. I snort.

"She is my *ĝha*. I cannot bother her."

"You can and you will. It is your nature," Hoga sighs. "She is unlike V`òllø women, and you can't treat her as such."

Annoyance flutters along my *jisa* like a shard of crystal stuck inside my shoe. I have waited for numerous moon cycles to meet my *ĝha,* and within hours of having her, I am told I am not permitted to see her. Surely, she will want to see me as I do her. Surely, her heart misses mine. Surely, I cannot bother her. I feel like a child being scolded by his mother. But I am Rogeshu. I can be chastised by no one.

"I think I will see her now," I say, going to step around Hoga. She moves with me, blocking my entrance into my *ĝha*'s space.

"She has not slept. Let her rest." Hoga tells me, glaring in my direction. I'm about to persist again when the one with the wild, flaming hair steps out of my *ĝha*'s room. Her eyes flick between Hoga and me before making a large circle with her pupils. The human female turns back to the room and slides through the beads. I hear her voice in their language, speaking with my *ĝha*. Then, I hear my *ĝha*.

"That's why I'm hiding." My *ĝha* says, and Blossom translates it beside me. My second heart stutters in my chest, momentarily choosing to beat differently than the first before shifting back to normal. I look into Hoga's eyes, and she arches an icy brow in my direction. Then, with a nod, I step away from the door.

"I will return to the village." I tell Hoga, "The people would like to hold a welcome feast for the women in two light cycles."

Pa's laughter grates on my nerves. Having been party to my rejection, he finds my suffering hilarious. He especially likes the part where Hoga glared so hard I left the loft with my tail between my legs like a fearful child.

"It's not funny." I insist, smacking his leg with my tail. Still, the *peholoe* chuckles, dancing out of the way of my attack. He is very spry for a *peholoe*. When his laughter dies, he finally provides his wisdom.

"You are a patient and faithful man, Kano. You have always known good things would come to you. Your *ĝha* will be no different if you choose to be no different."

I realize I sound petulant when I say, "But I have already waited."

The purple sand of the crystal fields crunches beneath our feet, creating a rhythmic, soothing sound. Since I had planned to spend the early slivers of the sun with my *ĝha*, I was free of duty to my people. Well, except Pa, who saw my distress and offered to accompany me for prayers.

"That is where you put your faith in the Baso Sheva and their plan, right? Did you not speak similar words to me of patience and faith mere moons ago? When we thought no *ĝhajo* existed and our people would not make it?"

"That is different," I say, though I know it is not. My *ĝha* is a beautiful creature. Captivating in her narrow frame and long hair the color of light beams. She draws my attention and makes my second heart beat erratically in my chest. The mere glimpse of her earlier was an exercise in self-control as I put her needs above mine. Providing for her and bringing her new foods to sample felt good. I wished I could have stayed to watch her taste; heard the pleasant hum she emits when she likes the food I bring. The memory of sharing fruit the day before kept me up through the night, imagining meals together alone in my home.

Pa does not argue with me. He only tilts his head down to sign respect and continues along the path. Together, we kneel in the shards and pray. I ask Baso Sheva for patience and thank her for the blessings of *ĝhajo*. She does not respond in resonance, but I still hear her answer. If I persist in tradition, my *ĝha* will deliver herself to me.

CHAPTER ELEVEN

"He's gone," Aston announces, prancing through the doorway. She has a wooden platter full of food, and my stomach growls. The last thing I ate was that fruit the night before and a half-ration from EP3 before that. Her plate seems to have some of that fruit, meat, bread, jam, and fish. She is snacking on a little bit of everything. *Everything Kano brought.*

When he arrived this morning, he smiled, staring right at me as he announced himself. I was so startled; I couldn't even move. One moment, I'm playing a game I hardly understand with the demanding Hoga. Then, the next, those eyes that penetrated my mind every time I blinked were suddenly there, locked on me like I was the world's biggest jewel. I half-expected him to pick me up and spin me around or drop his bag of goodies and run at me like the airport scene in a rom-com. But he didn't. He nodded to me gently and set breakfast up for everyone, giving me the perfect opportunity to disappear.

It wasn't that I was anti-falling-in-love-with-an-alien. It's that I was really hoping we would be able to make a return to Earth. I hoped this was a pit stop on our intergalactic cruise adventure. Plus, even if we did end up stuck on this planet for good, do I want the first alien to show any interest? What if there's some other chief right around the corner that's a better fit? You can't just declare someone your soulmate at first sight. It's not how it's done.

"Thanks," I get up from my bed and head toward the feast with Aston. When Kano brought the food, everyone was barely waking up, but now the *peholoe* loft was in full swing. The young children ran through the house playing tag underfoot, sneaking a bite of food on the way past the low table. The baby was asleep in Hoga's arms, softening out the alien woman's appearance. I didn't think that was possible. The twins and the older girl sat on the mats, discussing some show from back on Earth. And the women and Zach all huddled around the table, eating slowly and asking Blossom various questions about the planet and how to get off it.

"Blossom, didn't you say this place was only ninety-six percent hospitable?" Roxie asks, dipping some kind of bread in a liquid that looks suspiciously like coffee.

"Yes, this planet is ninety-six percent hospitable for human life." She says, nodding her assent.

I didn't have the opportunity to see Blossom's full-body mode yesterday, but I watched her curiously this morning. She was more advanced than any robot I'd seen on Earth, and her AI model was clearly cutting edge because there was a clear humanness to her mannerisms. She used common forms of body language as she spoke, keeping her metallic toes pointed toward the person she communicated with. Her glowing lilac eyes would focus on your face as she spoke. She would mirror your movements. It was beautiful and fascinating.

"Why?" Asks a woman with milky, unfocused eyes. She tucks her dark hair behind her ears and listens intently for Blossom's reply.

"The radiation levels of this planet are slightly higher than Earth's. Therefore, heat damage and stress are more likely to affect you. The locals seem to have a natural protectant against this."

"You're telling me I'm going to burn more easily? Big whoop. At least these people don't have dozens of eyes and freaking pincers." Roxie grumbles, choosing a meatball-like food at the center of the table.

"What about the V`òllø people? What can you tell us about them?" Zach asks, eyeing Hoga warily. Her eyes are narrowed on his, and her mouth is quirked slightly to the side. She is amused by his fear of her.

"As far as my scanners can tell, this village has 56 total living V`òllø, the majority of which are male or elders unable to reproduce."

"Sausage fest." Roxie snorts, making a couple of the other women giggle.

"How many women are there?" Zach asks. Roxie rolls her eyes. She must have woken up more like herself because this is the Roxie I remember from the ship.

Instead of Blossom answering, she translates for Hoga. "There are two unmated women in all of V`òllø. Soekho and Niore, but both are unmatchable. Trust the *peholoe*, we have tried."

Hoga sighs deeply as if she is relieved to give us this information. Her shoulders drop a slight amount as she looks across our group.

Blossom gives us the rest of the information, "They also have five married women and the women of the *peholoe*."

"What about other children?" Daria asks, looking at the small group of pre-teens flicking game chips at one another.

"There are six male V`òllø children," Hoga says, her lips thinning. It dawns on me then that this is why they are so excited by our arrival. This is why Kano said I was his soulmate. They need women, or their kind will die.

After cleaning up breakfast, Hoga put the baby down for a nap and then left to catch up with the rest of the *peholoe* on the ground. Before she left, she told us that they would host a grand feast for our arrival the next day. She told us the people – the men – of town wanted to meet us. They were curious about our arrival on this planet, which Hoga calls Shojo.

The women voice their true feelings about it when she's finally gone.

"There's no way it's safe," Roxie says, checking the rounds in her gun for the sixth time since Hoga left. She's one of the few women who chose the pants and tunic combo, using her belt from Earth to hold her holster.

"I agree," Daria adds, glancing at her younger sister. "It's probably some kind of trap."

"They've been friendly so far," Aston says tentatively.

"Because they need child-bearing women," Roxie snaps, her eyes scanning the loft for any kind of alien intruder.

"I don't know. I think it could be the V`òllø tradition. A way to make us feel more comfortable. That's all they've been trying to do since we got here," The blind woman, Clara, offers.

As the argument gets heated, I look around the room, and my eyes lock on Alba. She must have visited the bathhouse at some point because she looked as she did when I first met her, except without any makeup to brighten her naturally lovely complexion. Her lips are pursed in thought.

Interrupting a sharp jab from Roxie, I ask, "What do you think, Alba?"

Her head snaps up, her curls bouncing against her face lightly. I wasn't sure she even knew the topic of discussion until she answered.

"As far as my experience has taught, men who *want* women cannot be trusted," Roxie gets ready to tell everyone she told us so, but Alba continues, "But they are easily manipulated."

"What?" Roxie asks in disbelief.

"If these men know this planet better than anyone, we should use them to our advantage. Maybe they know of a way we can get off this planet. Or at the very least, we need them to be happy with us to ensure our survival."

"Blossom, what do you think?" I ask, trying to process Alba's unexpected words of wisdom. From my time on Earth, I knew about men who wanted women in the way she spoke of. I danced for them regularly and manipulated them into spending their money on my body. Then, when I started poker, I used all those hard lessons to manipulate my opponents. They liked to think I was inexperienced, weaker of mind, and more emotional than them. They all knew I had been a dancer. In fact, I had danced for some of them. And because they knew my body, they thought they knew my mind. So, they always seemed dumbfounded when I beat them out of house and home.

"The V`òllø are a friendly race, but they are also warriors. The statistical likelihood of human manipulations resulting in a positive outcome is lower than I would suggest acting on. Furthermore, the V`òllø people do not have technologies like our planet. They would have no information on how we can return to Earth."

"What is our statistical likelihood of returning to Earth?" Aston asks, hope brims in her voice.

"Eight-point-two percent."

The energy in the room dips. With the escape pod still smashed up against the bay, Blossom's expertise, and the messages the *SS Herculean* had sent to Earth during the attack, I had been counting on a savior. Another human ship was coming after the *SS Herculean,* and they would find the information from the escape pod, and they would come and save us. It's the story I had spun in my sleepless nights on the pod. And it seemed like I hadn't been the only one.

"Can we improve that?" I ask, my voice barely a whisper.

Blossom's voice is businesslike when she says, "No, all major factors of improvement are outside of our control."

"Great," Roxie grumbles, stuffing another bite of food into her face. "Operation Alien Brides it is."

CHAPTER TWELVE

The creepy caw of a bird jars me from my sleep. I glance over to the other bed in our room, and Aston isn't there. Outside, the sun sets in the sky, painting it shades of maroon. A stripe of lime shimmers between the unnatural purple color and the deep warm color of their night sky. Stars are already visible, speckling the impending darkness. I couldn't have been asleep for more than an hour, the view outside was almost identical when I finally crashed, but I felt rested. The odd hissing and buzzing sounds outside fade into the background as I hear the women's bustle in the loft's central area.

Pulling myself from bed, I stretch to my toes and feel my back crackle. I wasn't quite ready to change to alien wear, so I washed my clothes in the bathhouse and slept in one of the scratchy linen tunics. Feeling my jeans, I was pleasantly surprised to find them dry, except along the ankle hems. Slipping into my outfit, I went out to visit with the other women.

"Oh, Vera! Good. We weren't sure you were ever going to wake up." Alba says, rushing to my side. She's dressed in an alien gown, different than the day dress she wore this morning. This gown covered her way down to her toes. It was belted at the waist with a latch made of bright-red crystal. Her curls are pulled back from her face, and she has a red stain on her lips.

"I couldn't have been asleep that long," I grumble, still trying to banish the grogginess of my nap.

Aston rolls her eyes at me, "Vee, you slept all the way through the day. We're due for dinner at dark. Hoga and the *Peholoe* are coming to escort us in *two slivers of the sun.*"

She uses the term in mocking as if she found it in some old Renaissance classic rather than from the lips of Hoga. Her voice is hoity-toity, and I wonder if she's emulating the grouchy elder. I want to laugh, but then my brain registers what she told me. I'd slept through the entire day. I hadn't been asleep for an hour but a whole day.

"Why didn't anyone wake me?" I ask, incredulity and concern creasing my brow.

"Because you needed it after gambling away the night," Aston says, slipping crystal earrings she'd fashioned from her simple gold studs into her ears.

She looked fantastic. Her dress was the color of a dark monstera plant. It wrapped around her body to be cinched at her waist, accentuating her curvaceous form. She wore sandals underneath, and her curls were voluptuous and wild around her head. She wore the same red color as Alba on her lips, but it appeared brighter against paler skin.

I look from her to Alba, who nods in agreement. Then, I sweep around the room. All of the women are dressed to the nines except Daria. Like me, she wears her human clothes. Unlike me, she still looks good. Even after the wash, my clothes hold the stain of alien blood spatter. Sure, they smelled like eucalyptus and mint to my human nose, but at the scent of my arrival, Kano had decided I was his soulmate. Who knew what he would be able to scent on my clothes.

I consider changing like everyone else, but Hoga and the other peholoe arrive before I get the chance. Looks like I'm wearing jeans to the welcome dinner. Worse, the *peholoe* didn't come alone. Standing beside Hoga, Kano stands looking every bit the alien leader he is.

CHAPTER THIRTEEN

My *ĝha* is a curious creature. She says she does not lead the women, but her thoughts turn back to them as constantly as my own toward my village. She acted as if she wanted to walk ahead with her tribe, but she slowed her feet as we approached the tribal hut, sticking close to my side. This pleased and confused me. Now, she sits between me and her fire-haired friend, Az-ton, who tucks a white bean in her hand. I'm curious, but my *ĝha* places it in her pocket and startles when she realizes my attention is on her.

All of my people are excited about the arrival of human females and children. Their energy seems to buzz through the room, strengthening my *jisa*. Rihu placed himself between Az-ton and Royi, and my *ĝha*'s friend did not seem interested in his playful antics. Nor does the bright female beside Royi. Llazho glares across the table at Az-ton's polite smiles, and I see his jaw clench. Fury akin to learning he lost his day's fish crackles along his *jisa,* and I wonder if his heart recognizes my *ĝha*'s closest friend.

Meanwhile, the rest of the humans are tentatively getting along with my people, though they seem nervous. The *peholoe* have scattered amongst the humans, except for Hoga, who still sits beside me, criticizing how I sit and chew. I find it curious that she does the same to my *ĝha*, tossing mild taunts her way. Pa, seated further down the table, seems to be getting along with the human, Alba. She and her daughter have spins in their hair, and the nursling only seems to cease its cry when Pa is nearby. Finally, Gowi and Jigu sit with the sun-thetic smarts, Blossom. They like to learn about my *ĝha*'s home planet's customs, asking the metallic creature dozens of questions. Many of the answers I find odd.

Rra is silent beside a quiet human with bright spins of hair. A child that looks almost exactly like the human sits on her other side, peering at Rra curiously. Twin boys annoy the only human adult male as he eats, but he does not lash out at them or act like a parent. So, I assume he has never had a *ĝha* of his own. I guess they are his kin.

When the moon finally rises, the food is served. Traditional V`òllø stew is pulled from the centerfire and placed on a cloth at the center of the table. Then, it is surrounded by the many sides and sweets my people prepared. Salads of greens and roots, bright fruit tarts, grains of *llige*, and warm slices of bread surround the pot. Shallow wooden bowls are passed down the table, and my men jump at the opportunity to serve the human women. I wish to do the same for my *ĝha*.

"May I serve you?" I ask, my hand crawling toward her dish. My Vera nods, turning back to Az-ton as I take her plate. Carefully, I create a wall with the *llige,* serving a spoonful of stew to the side. Next, I pile some of the best salads and bread in the clean, fresh part of her bowl. Then, I place an *uni* fruit tart on the flat ledge. Only when I am content with the food on her plate do I set it before her and serve myself.

As I eat, enjoying the flavors of my village, I can't help but feel the presence of the Baso Sheva. Her blessings are abundant among us. My *ĝha* and her friend speak of the food, comparing the *llige* to a food called wild rice. I want to explain that it is a grain and cannot be wild. It's cultivated in the farms along the bay, but instead, I listen to my Vera's soft voice.

Soon enough, their topics turn to other things and then nothing as the sky warriors pull Az-ton's attention from my *ĝha*. They are clearly amused by her fiery head spins and expressive eyes. On the other hand, My Vera is more reserved in her expressions, keeping her feelings inside while perceiving the situation around her.

Her eyebrows crinkle momentarily when Hoga whispers, "Speak now, Kano."

I stand, looking between Blossom, my *ĝha*, and the *peholoe*. My hearts beat quicker in my chest as the table goes silent. My people look towards me, placing down their feasting utensils. And the humans follow suit, fixing their eyes on Blossom for her translated words.

"My people, thank the Baso Sheva today with this meal. As she answered my prayers and brought us *ĝhajo*." My people, with their decorated horns, pat their thighs in celebration. The humans seem more comfortable now that they have eaten, and they listen closely to Blossom's words. "Please treat them with the utmost honor and kindness, and one of them could be your *ĝha*, as Vera is mine."

I look down at my beautiful *ĝha*. Her eyes are wide, displaying her sea-colored eye circles, and I think I have pleased her with my words. Her lips part with a breath, and I wait for her to tell me she is my *ĝha*, but she only stares. I watch as her chest rises and falls and wonder if her hearts beat in tune with mine. I attune my ears to the sound but only hear a singular tune in her chest. My brows furrow, and I turn away from my *ĝha* to finish my speech.

"This night, we celebrate, and the next, we shall start a festival of many days that will end in our *R̈uṣad'ù*. D'o go chu merchu, Baso Sheva."

My people repeat my words as the humans stare wide-eyed and open-mouthed. I believe they bask in the pleasure of the upcoming celebration.

CHAPTER FOURTEEN

This can't be happening. If Blossom's translation was correct, Kano said we are marrying at the end of the week. The aliens are all looking at me like I'm the one ring to rule them all – Kano especially. The light of the central fire glints off his horns like the sparkle in a teeth-whitening commercial, and my heart picks up the pace. This excites him further because he tries to smile at me, revealing a few sharp teeth among normal incisors.

My eyes flash between Aston, who is too busy glaring at another alien across the table to notice my eyes begging, 'Help me,' and Blossom, who waves me off like this isn't some major cultural miscommunication. I've been doing my best to keep my emotions close to the vest, but I can't very well stay complacent and let something like this happen. *Right?* Right.

I slam my palms down on the table and stand, baring my teeth before shoving my way out of the tribal meeting hut. I don't know what an alien looks like startled, but I imagine that's the feeling Kano has as he watches me storm away. My outburst seems to get Aston's attention, and I hear her call my name, but she doesn't follow me.

Outside, the moon is bright in the sky, and I realize then that there are two of them. One is closer and brighter, and the other is slightly off-center of the first and much further away. It looks smaller that way. Regardless, they are both full and provide plenty of light for me to navigate back to the karst. Tonight, Alba said it would be easier to stay on the ground. She was worried about the children getting too close to the edges, but the *peholoe* said there was plenty of space for both the *peholoe* and the humans and that they would be happy to help with the children. With the *peholoe*'s eyes, Alba conceded. Regardless, that's the only place I felt I had any control over, and I would be spending as much time there and away from Kano as I could.

I can hear footsteps behind me, and when I glance over my shoulder, I see his big, hulking dark green frame. He looks even darker in the moonlight, and his silver tattoos seem to shine. He's dressed in a flowy shirt and a sharp jacket, and my mind conjures the image of him yesterday when he tore his soaked shirt from his carved abs. *Carved abs? What is happening to you, Vera?*

Shaking my head, I try to dislodge the weird thoughts of attraction and focus on tearing open the gate to the chasm area. From the tour, I knew this place was dangerous in the daylight and worse in the night. I could see why. The mushrooms glowed, making the shadows of the chasm deeper and less clear. The bridge over the top had no light of its own, so I had to trust that following the path would lead me across the bridge. I felt the rough, scratchy rope under my hands and carefully climbed a couple of steps to the bridge. My human eyes did little to help me navigate the darkness.

"Ja Vera, go. Go!" Kano says from way too close behind me. I want to scream at him and tell him that yes, I go. So, he should leave me alone, but I spin too fast, and my leg catches on the rope before I accidentally sling myself backward off the bridge and into the chasm. Adrenaline is like a bullet in my veins as its icy panic whips through me, and I reach out to catch on to... something. Anything. I feel a ledge, and I clasp on for dear life. Digging my fingernails into the edge, I feel my wrist pop and my palm stretch along the rough rock. Despite living in earth's warm, rocky places, I had never rock climbed in my life. The fact that life now hung on my capability to pull myself out of the chasm in the dark sent fearful thoughts racing through my mind.

My fingertips were curled and clawed into the tiny ledge, and my mind was like a runaway train of bad juju.

Images of falling off the rope in middle-school gym class and cartoons where the characters' fingers slip one by one until they fall to their doom swirl in my mind. The idea of falling only brings forth middle-schoolers laughing and the comedic splat of a mischievous animal, and an unsettling giggle bursts out of my chest. I try to pull myself up, feeling my forearms burn and my back quake. I try to find a foothold in the wall from feeling alone but waving my feet back and forth makes my shoulders burn.

Bright side is that looking down, all my human eyes can see is blackness, so I have no idea how far I would drop until I died. Less bright side, when I look up, I can barely see the light for the opening, which means I am a little further down than I hoped. At this moment, I really wished I had been a rock climber. The stage never prepared me for something like this.

"Ja Vera! Ja Vera!" Kano's panicked yells finally reach my ears, and I have to wonder how long he's called my name. My whole upper body burns, but I'm holding steady.

"Kano? I'm here. Please help!" I shout back, wondering if he will understand the plea in my voice. I left Blossom with the rest of the humans at dinner, and the tiny earbud Aston gave me was tucked safely in my pocket. This means we get to raw dog language in this (hopefully) hero moment.

"D'o hi nu e!" He says though it's absolute gibberish to me. I hope that means he's got some rope or something to lasso me with. I look up, and a torchlight sets his face in shadow. I watch him put the torch beside him, and I have to wonder what it's made of to be placed along the wood without burning it. Then, I watch him drop down to hang off the edge of the bridge.

"Wait! No. No!" I shout as he swings back and forth before catching a foot on the wall and crouching alongside it.

"J'e. D'o no A." He says back, climbing down further with a grunt. He's a shadow along the cliff face, and I watch as he carefully places his hands and feet along the rocky wall. I realize how awful this cavern is when he gets to about five feet above me. I'm lucky to have found a place to hold on. The part of the cavern he clings to overhangs the part I'm clinging to. This means he would have to find a safe way under the overhang to get me and then, somehow, bring us both back up. He hikes sideways, coming closer until his voice is much nearer. He seems to speak to me soothingly.

My arms burn with strain as I search the walls for a way to get out of this hole alive. If only we had a rope or something. As I'm about to tell him to get Aston or ask for help, the chasm shakes, and the stability of my left hand becomes questionable at best. Kano is close enough now that I can see him look beyond me, and the color of his eyes drains. Crawling my fingers carefully back into place, my whole upper body burns. Still, I turn my neck as far as possible, and a deluge of fear overtakes me.

I want to run, but I can't. I'm hanging from the side of a cliff with nowhere to run, nowhere to turn. So, instead, I freeze. My impending scream is caught in my throat, and my joints lock in place as I hang. Everything seems to come into great focus as I look over my shoulder at the terrifying creature behind me. It would be kind of like an octopus if an octopus had goat-like horns and armored tentacles. It scrambles over the rock silently, and the hundred-slitted glowing eyes stare back at me. My heart beats a violent rhythm in my chest, and without moving my head, I glance back at Kano. He has slowly begun climbing back away, and my beating heart drops. *Is he going to abandon me to the monster? I thought I was his soulmate!*

As if hearing my thoughts, he stops his movement. Looking down at me, he sends me a wink and disappears into the darkness. *Ass!* The moment feels suspended in time. I don't move; I barely breathe. One of the monster's many tentacles reaches forward, and I prepare myself to climb. But my limbs refuse to move, my exhaustion weighs me down, and frustration fires through me. I refused to die a gruesome tentacled death. I'd fall first.

Then, the *swhip* of an arrow skips past my head, and I hear the beast roar behind me. The end of the shaft sticks out of the outstretched tentacle, and fire seems to burn from its end, making my eyes widen in horror. I watch as the beast's many eyes lock onto the origin of the arrow, and mine follow. Kano stands there, grinning like a madman, as he lets another arrow fly.

CHAPTER FIFTEEN

I cannot let the *jachepod* reach my sweet Vera. The monster of the chasm has claimed one too many beautiful females in its time. I just found My Vera, and I would not be a good partner if I let her die so swiftly upon her arrival. This is a test from the Baso Sheva, and I will face it with honor. Whistling through my teeth, I get the attention of the *jachepod* and my mount, Lewe. I draw another arrow and let it fly as the *jachepod's* many eyes land on me. The fire-crystal head tears through the crumbly armor and into the squishy flesh beneath.

I do not know what I have said to offend my sweet Vera. Whatever it was, she surely did not need to throw herself over the edge of the chasm bridge to prove all I would do for her. I am man enough to know that a simple apology is more befitting. Even so, this is where we find ourselves.

My mount is quick to respond, flying to the bridge behind me and lowering his neck for me to mount. Unfortunately, it will not be me riding today. I have to push back the beast. My darling Vera, my very soul, however, hangs below the overhang and out of my reach. But not Lewe's. Whistling in the tune of his kind, I point my horns toward My Vera. His beady eyes lock on her, and a slight twinge of unnecessary jealousy pangs through me. *He is my mount, and he will save her. So, what if he gets to hold her before I do. She will be alive because of him.*

I let another arrow fly; this one aimed for the beast's center. Somewhere in the *jachepod's* armored jelly, its heart floats about dodging my arrows. Lewe caws loudly, and I glance over at him to see my Vera gently clasped in his claws. She didn't scream like I would have imagined, but rather her beautiful eyes were pressed tightly closed, and her hands dug into the clawed feet of Lewe. Diving low, they brush across the mushrooms, and I worry about Vera's reaction. Blossom said that it could be harmful. Still, Lewe pauses in the air waiting for more directions, and I whistle out an answer carefully. I want Lewe to take her to the *peholoe*'s loft and then notify the warriors I need their help at the bridge. Much more intelligent than one might think, Lewe doesn't hesitate to fly my *sodza* to the loft.

I keep shooting my arrows, knowing I only have ten. The *jachepod* climbs higher, bringing himself into the light and to a disadvantage. The creatures of the chasm hide there because the depth is so low darkness invades every corner. During the day, they do not come so high, but during the night... My fifth arrow flies.

The rowdy steps of my men come behind me, and I hear the feminine gasp of a human. As the *jachepod* comes into the light, the moon illuminates the heart within its body, and my arrow aims. Before I can release it, a boom like thunder explodes from the gates, and I watch the glowing edges of the heart explode outward under the natural armor that becomes translucent in the light. The *jachepod* screeches before falling from the ledge. Moments later, a horrible crunch echoes from the chasm.

I look at the group gathered around. The woman who stood beside my Vera at their arrival packs away her black metal weapon with a huff. Az-ton pushes her aside and shouts, "Where is she? Where is Vera?"

Blossom translates when I say, "She's safe."

CHAPTER SIXTEEN

The creepy mega-crow drops me at the island's edge beside the *peholoe*'s tree house. He caws at me, glaring in my direction like a rebuke. It's not like I wanted to fall off the side of the bridge. I wasn't usually clumsy, but being here pushed me far past my comfort zone. I may never be the old Vera again. Glancing down at my body, I notice the blue powder that dusts the mushrooms has gathered like pollen on my shirt, and I dust it off with my palm in disgust before I remember Blossom's word of warning. *Oops.*

Thinking about washing it off, I go to the bathhouse and strip out of my dirty clothes. The translation earbud Aston gave me falls from my pocket, and I push it into my ear in case I hear an alien coming. The room still smells minty and fresh as I step into the waters. It's hot, but not unbearably so. And as my feet sink beneath the water, I groan in pleasure, feeling my tension drift away.

Further and further in, I go until I'm skimming the surface with outstretched arms and dunking beneath it to feel the warmth in the edges of my hair. Finally, all the tension seems to ease from my body, and I can't imagine why I was so frustrated less than an hour ago that I had to storm from dinner like a hothead. I was *good* at keeping my emotions close to the vest, but my behavior at dinner was so unlike me.

My body seems to thaw from the cool night air, and I hum a moan of appreciation. Every nerve-ending feels like it's bathed in Vicodin, and I loosen further. The thought comes unbidden to my mind. *Kano looked so hot defending me.*

I imagine the flex of his arms against the draw of his bow and that intense gaze on me. Heat pools below my belly, and my nipples peak beneath the water. I crouch lower and glide back toward one of the stone seats along the edge. Soft moonlight and glowing stones bathe the room in soft light, and the way the water caresses my body makes me think of the warmth of his hands. Muscled, veined hands with surprisingly human fingers that could look incredible gripping onto my hips as he —

What are you thinking? My mind reprimands me, but the heat doesn't leave my belly, and the unthinking part of me wants to sink into the fantasy. Glancing both ways, I imagine everyone is still at dinner or helping Kano with the terrible mess I've made. If I played a little, no one would ever know. *It's stress relief.*

I start slow, drawing my hand over my chest, gently drawing circles around my peaked nipple. It wrests another moan from my chest, and the humble vibrations spark straight to the peak of my thighs. My clit throbs, and I can't remember the last time I ever felt this way — maybe never. The water laps around me gently as one hand moves across my chest to give the same attention to my other nipple. My eyes close in pleasure, and my head tilts against the stone floor.

Slowly crawling my other hand down my flat belly, I glide a finger along my seam, feeling my own wetness. As much as I wanted to blame it on the steamy water, I knew better. This was because that ridiculously hot alien plagues my mind on this ridiculously alien planet. Even as my finger separates my lower lips, I think of his ridiculously handsome face. Those jade eyes seemed to sear into me every time they looked, and I could only imagine their intensity on me watching *this.*

Circling my clit, I imagine him standing there across the room. His eyes are so engulfed in color he can hardly hold back, but he does because I won't let him do anything but watch. I imagine his fists clenched at his sides, his cock growing in his pants, pressing against the ties at the front. I wonder what his cock looks like. I envision a cock that is green and ribbed with silver. My pussy clenches at the thoughts. I imagine it's big – bigger than I'd ever seen. I bet it has a vein that throbs at the sight of my lips parted on a moan.

I can practically hear his grumbly voice, telling me in his gibberish language that I'm a good girl. That I should come all over those long, strong fingers. Biting my lip, the heat pools and my muscles tighten. I imagine him saying, "Come for me, my Vera." And I do. Everything tightens and spasms, and an overtly sexual moan splits my lips. I wait for myself to come down like a crash, but it doesn't happen.

The energy in the room seems to electrify, and my body is left completely unsatisfied. My eyes flash open in frustration, and my lips part in a gasp. Kano is standing right there, eyes pinpointed on me, lips parted in a half-growl. My hand mindlessly teases my nipple, and I rip it from my chest, grabbing the sides of the bench beneath the water. I lick my lips, and my eyes dart side to side. No one else is in the bathhouse, but I can hear the soft discussions of the *peholoe* and the women outside. It sounds like I ended the party, and they're talking about where everyone will sleep.

Even with the normalcy of the conversation outside, my blood is heated, and the way his eyes rake down my flushed, naked body only boils me further.

His voice is gruff, demanding. The translation rings clear as day, "Don't stop, my Vera."

My eyes lock onto his as my hands find their places once again. One teasing my nipples, the other circling my clit. Somewhere in the back of my mind, I can feel the real Vera banging on the door of her cage, begging to get out. She wouldn't be doing this. But then, Kano groans, and his hands clenched so tight I think he will break them. Whatever *is* in his pants presses against the seams, and I want to see it.

I don't recognize my voice as I say, "Show me."

He doesn't hesitate. Unclenching one fist, he singlehandedly draws the laces open and fists his pulsing cock. It's better than I imagined. A thick silver vein presses against the slightly curved underside and leads to a broad, flared head. Instead of ribbing along the sides, a triangle of bumps sits above his dick instead of hair. A glistening drop of precum beads on top of the head. I moan. His thighs flex, and I want to ride him. But, even in my lusty haze, I recognize how crazy that is and choose to keep my distance.

"My Vera." He grunts, twisting his fist up his shaft before stroking back down to the base.

My mind is like a runaway train. Now that I've seen Kano's cock, it's all I can think about. My hands move effortlessly, and images flash through my mind. Me on my knees before him, licking up that beautiful silver vein before swirling the thick head in my mouth. Him underneath me as I slowly lower my pink wetness over him, grinding against his bumps. Me on all fours underneath him as he powers his cock into me over and over and over. My fingers slip inside me, pumping as I watch his hand on his cock.

He groans at the sight, and I want him closer. If only he were a little closer. My eyes tilt shut, and I try to pretend my fingers are his length. They've snapped open again at his growled command.

"Look at me."

Locking those beautiful jade orbs with mine. Together we grow louder until I'm coming again all over my fingers. He jerks into his fist, and a rope of silver, iridescent cum stripes his hand and the tiles in front of him. *I want to lick him clean.* It's that thought that finally shakes me. I orgasmed in front of an alien. I fantasized about an alien. Worse yet, I still wanted the alien. And from the look on his face, he knows it.

CHAPTER SEVENTEEN
Kano

My *ĝha*'s chest rises and falls erratically as she springs from the water on the opposite end of the pool. A groan leaves me at the sight of the droplets of water caressing her sweet curves in the same ways I wish to. The ends of her hair drip to the tile, and I'm frozen in place by her beauty. I'm sure my eyes are so overtaken with color that there is nothing but green. I take a step forward, and she takes a step back. I take a step to the left, and she takes a step further away. Is this a game? Does she want a chase?

"Kano." She sounds so stern in the little ear bean Az-ton gave me, but that only pleases me more. I can hear the low growl starting in my chest. Her eyes flick to my cock, then back to my face, and I smirk. She wants me. I take another step toward her. She takes another step away. My smirk drops.

"What is this, my pretty soul?" I ask, taking another step to watch her step away. "I will chase you if you like."

Her eyes widen slightly, and she glances around the room for some kind of escape. The *peholoe*'s bathhouse only has two exits and both of which would require her to pass me. I would capture her easily. Instead, I watch her beautiful sea-blue eyes lock on her filthy clothes. Looking at me one last time, she scurries over to them and pulls the shirt over her head. Confusion pinches my brows.

"That is filthy," I say, taking another step toward her. She steps away once again, and I growl in frustration. I move much faster than her, and I stand before her in only a few strides. Her dirt-scuffed pants are held in front of her, and her smell perfumes the air. I grab her pants from her, but she does not release them. Another growl escapes me. "You can't wear those."

She smacks the back of my hand, and I release the pants with surprise. My tiny *ĝha* hisses, "I can wear whatever I please."

Tilting my head down to hers, I ask, "It pleases you to wear clothing that smells of monsters and *d'oru*?"

"It pleases me to wear my own clothes." She mumbles, sticking one of her beautiful pale legs through the hole. The wet strands of her hair dampen her white shirt, and my eyes lock on the hint of skin beneath it.

"I can have your clothes cleaned. I have clean ones you can borrow." I offer, dragging my eyes up to hers though every part of me begs to tear her tiny shirt from her chest and tease her pink buds between my teeth. She latches her pants and tries to step away from me, but I reach out and pull her toward me instead.

"Kano." She warns, but I will not hear it. I bury my face in her neck, inhaling softly. My cock thickens in my trousers at her scent. She smells like fresh rain and night-root flowers with a hint of something homey. She freezes against me, and I try to place that final hint of scent. Helleboralis.

I step back so quickly that she sways. I catch her arm to stabilize her, and my apologies cannot come quick enough.

"Apologies, My Soul. I did not realize you were sick. Let me help you."

"Sick?" she murmurs, wringing some of the water out of her hair. "I'm not sick."

"But you must have touched the Helleboralis fungi. They make your blood heat; they make you sick."

Realization covers her face, and she looks at the blue powder dusting her white shirt. A spattering of pink covers her cheeks, and I wonder if her blood is heating. She again tears her shirt from her body before scrambling back into the water. Her pants become a dark blue, and she sticks her hands inside the holes on the sides, pinching her lips together. They are oddly cute, her trousers. They cling to her upper leg and flare much wider than her lower leg at the bottom.

I strip my shirt from my back and offer it to Vera with an outstretched hand. It is much larger than her tiny scrap of fabric, and she could wear it without her sopping trousers. Now that I know she is ill, my desire dies in my chest. The only wish I have now is that My Soul feels better. I tell her as much, but the same hazy look from earlier takes over her eyes. Guilt pinches in my chest. I didn't realize she was not feeling well earlier. I saw her body, free of her restrictive clothes, and wanted to see what would happen.

"My Vera, please get out of the water. You need to be warm and dry." I plead, stepping closer to the edge of the pool. I think the *peholoe* have sorted out the sleeping arrangements because the discussion outside has taken on a much quieter tone, and I cannot hear the tittering of children.

Vera splashes me with a kick of water from her tiny toes, and I rip the dry shirt away with a growl. Her eyes are alight, and I narrow my own.

"Why don't you come in, Kano?" She purrs, sweeping her hand over her breast. I clench my jaw, feeling my *jisa* shake. I send up a prayer of strength to the Baso Sheva. Then, I shake my horns to the left.

I step away from the pool, and Vera whimpers her disappointment. Keeping my eyes on My Soul, I stand with my arms crossed.

"Kano," Vera whines, carrying out the final syllable of my name. My eyes find hers, and I watch a pout come to her lips. Lucious lips I want to bite but cannot because she is sick, and until she is better, she can't make that decision.

"Come out of the water, My Soul." I urge, showing her the clean shirt once again.

The lap of the water draws my attention, and I see Vera crawl out of the water at my feet. I worry about her dainty knees on the stone and practically beg her to stand.

She does as I ask, and instead of letting her advance, I spin her into my chest. The warmth of her body is a balm to my soul, but the slight tinge of sour Helleboralis in the room reminds me this is not a *ĝha's* embrace. Tugging my shirt collar over her head, I unfurl the rest of the fabric until it sits above her knees. Her lips are pursed in a pout, and she slides a hand over my bare chest. Grasping it in my own, I inspect her five tiny fingers. They are thin and pointier than my own. Her nails are a whitish pink, whereas mine are silver and black. What I find most noticeable is how good her hand looks in mine. It's so much smaller.

Her beautiful blue eyes peer up at me, and I send a rattle down my *jisa* to distract myself. I have much to discuss with Baso Sheva.

I see the moment the poison fades and the exhaustion takes over. As far as I know, that was Vera's second wave. Her third will happen sometime at night, and I pray the Baso Sheva lets her tiny human body sleep through it. Her eyes, previously filled with lust, are now drowsy and droopy. Her head rests against my chest, and my hearts pick up a synchronized beat.

"I'm sleepy," she murmurs. She snuggles against me. "You're warm."

Sweeping her into my arms, I nuzzle against her and whisper gently, "Sleep."

I carry her out to the seating area, and the *peholoe* all sit around playing a silent game of Neked'I with their tiny carved chips. Pa is the first to look up, but he immediately averts his eyes, putting them back on his game. I am glad to see he is back to his usual antics.

As is Hoga. "You should bring her home."

"This is her home," I say, waiting for them to point me to her room. We all know she would stay with me in time, but humans are still new to our world. Pa made a good point when he said they do not yet know of our customs. I'm trying to pay attention to my beloved soulmate, but my ears catch on Llazho growling outside. The *peholoe* must hear it, too, because they pause to listen.

Llazho's low voice carries throughout the treehouse. "Az-ton! Why do you sit with Rihu?"

Her response comes, and the incredible ear bean translates her response.

"I already told you, I sat next to Vera! I don't even know who Rihu is."

Llazho's growly responses are clearer than Az-ton's soft voice, "This is important."

Az-ton sighs, and I cannot tell what this means. The humans seem to sigh from pleasure and annoyance and tiredness. It does not help me at all to decode their conversation. Not that it matters when Az-ton stomps through the entry to find my very sleepy *ĝha* in my arms.

"What are you doing?" The fire-haired woman snaps, seeing Vera wearing only my shirt and lying tucked in my arms.

"Putting My Vera to bed," I respond, stepping toward the room she shares with Az-ton. I did not want to enter in case Az-ton was already sleeping, but since she was not, I stepped toward the room. Then, I am halted by Hoga.

"A *ĝha*'s home is with their *ĝha*. If she wakes here alone, it will affect her." Hoga says, playing with her chips and sending Rra into a panic.

"The humans do not seem to react the same to the bond," I argue, looking at Az-ton's narrowed eyes. "Maybe she would be better off here."

"She would," Az-ton argues, glaring at Hoga when the *peholoe* makes her next order.

"Take the female home," Hoga demands, winning their current round in the same breath. I look at the other *peholoe*, and they all nod in agreeance. Az-ton only glares at me. I second-guess my own wisdom because it is a rare day when all the *peholoe* agree on anything.

Looking to my *ĝha*, I see her lashes flutter, and a soft moan leaves her lips as she cuddles into me further. Az-ton is obviously unhappy with the proposed arrangement, but I want to stay the night with my *ĝha*. I only worry about her reaction. Reinforcing my *jisa*, I nod to the *peholoe*.

"She will be at my home along the cliffside," I tell Az-ton. "You can come to her at first light."

Then, I take my *ĝha* to bed.

CHAPTER EIGHTEEN

I fling my leg over my body pillow and groan in satisfaction. It was all a dream. No awful space cruise, no alien attack, no crash-landing on a nice-alien planet. I crack open one eye, and the sun's light streams in through a wall of windows. I notice the frame is not the slick black of my own, and my brows furrow. My eyes trail down the wall and to the wooden floor. It's dusty in here. As my eyes continue their journey, my heart falls in my chest. This isn't home at all.

Big, green, and muscled, Kano's chest rises and falls softly beneath me. My leg is slung over his tree trunk of a thigh, and embarrassment washes through me. I don't want to know how long I've been cuddled up to him, why his bed is so incredibly comfortable, or why I don't want to move. Carefully, I draw my eyes up his body and to his face.

When we first landed on the planet, they looked so huge and menacing, probably colored by our first alien experience. And the fact that they are huge with horns and weapons. Now, Kano seems different. His thick brows are relaxed, and his lips are slightly parted. His jaw is slack, and one of his hands rests beside his head. He draws in a low, even breath, and I decide I can escape this.

First, I plan to carefully move my leg. Looking at the predicament, I almost gasp at our size difference. I'm not short by any means, coming in at six foot one, and my friends in school used to call me 'legs.' Still, my leg wrapped around his barely covers him from hip to thigh. I think the best plan is to lift the whole leg and hover rather than sliding off the way I slid on. So, that's what I do.

Peeking up at his face, he still draws in low, even breaths. Next is my body. Pushing my hips back away from his side, I hear a slight grumble and freeze. He's still asleep when I look, so I move on to the next part, my upper body. One hand is tucked close to my chest, against his side, and the other is flung over his pec, hand splayed out wide. My head rests against his bicep. *Is that what it's called on an alien? A bicep?*

Using my bottom arm, I prepare to push myself into a sitting position. When I'm finally ready, I make one last check on Kano to make sure he's sleeping, and sure enough –

He's not.

Those captivating eyes are open and staring at me. I've got one leg propped up and my hips pushed back, with a hand pressed hard into the bed while my other is half lifted over his chest. I look ridiculous. His shirt from the night before starts slipping down my thigh, and my eyes widen in panic. I force myself into a seated position, chuckling awkwardly as I scramble away from his massive chest. I'm practically crab-walking backward when he sits up, and my eyes widen. My foot kicks his elbow on accident, and I wince as I push myself further away.

"Uh, em, sorry. I was trying not to wake you – oh!" I screech as I go tumbling over the edge of his bed and onto the wooden slats of the floor. I land on my back. Clenching my eyes closed, I bring my hands to cover them further. When I peek between my fingers, he's on all fours leaning over the edge of the bed to peer at me.

I'm not met with the disgust or curiosity I expect; instead, it's concern. Kano's eyes search mine to ensure I'm not rattled. Then, they trail over my body searching for injury. Finally, he reaches down and curls me back onto the bed. He speaks when I sit before him, my arms wrapped around my knees.

"Did you sleep well, My Vera?"

I don't trust myself to speak, so I nod. I realize that this takes Kano a moment to decipher, and the silence spreads as he thinks through what my nod might mean. Finally, when he's confident he understands, he leans forward and places his palm by my hip, his thumb brushing it gently.

"Do you feel like yourself again?" His morning voice is huskier than his normal one, and my heart pitter-patters in my chest at the earthy gravel in his tone. I nod shortly, and a soft groan leaves him. His lips dip towards mine, and I can't help it as my head tilts toward his. I remember some things about last night, and with him leaning over me like this, I can't think of anything I want more than to feel Kano's lips on mine.

He gets so close my eyes flutter shut. And then, three sharp bangs rattle beyond the far wall before Aston stomps in dressed like an alien princess.

"Oh, good hell, not you too." She harrumphs, finding me in this very compromising position. Kano huffs, but a smile tilts his lips as he exits the bed. The whole mattress shifts without him in it and one of my hands falls to the mattress to steady me.

"I will be outside, My Vera."

Blossom comes whirring into the room behind Aston. I twirl toward my best friend and hang my feet off the edge of the bed. She looks beautifully put together. A long linen dress, the color of corn husks, drapes over her slim frame, and a woven belt with red and blue crystals sewn throughout ties at the front of her hips. Her red hair is partially braided in a coronet, while the rest tumbles down her back in soft curls. Blossom is sparkling and pink; her lavender eyes glow as she joins us. I look down at myself and feel disgusted.

"Tell me you didn't sleep with him. We're meant to be getting off this damn planet, not the locals."

"The statistical likelihood of a return to Earth is less than two percent," Blossom adds, momentarily making Aston glare in her direction.

"How about you tell Vera here about what has happened since she tried to throw herself into the chasm instead of crushing my dreams? Yeah?" It's directed at Blossom, but Aston raises her brow at me.

I sigh. "Blossom, please report what has happened since I left the welcome dinner."

"Would you like that in order of priority or chronologically?" She asks, blinking clunkily.

"Let's go with priority."

"Last night, the V`òllø recognized many new soulmates, including Zhu for Cerridwen, Niore for Lucia, and Llazho for —
"

"Move on." Aston snaps, glaring at the robot. Blossom doesn't mind her snippiness, moving to the next part of her report with ease.

"The brothers Zachary, Cain, and Abel have been invited by the warriors to train with them. They will head toward the training grounds shortly." Blossom pauses, waiting for me to comment, and I try to gather my thoughts quickly.

"Cain and Abel are just children."

"Warriors here train from childhood in case of war," Blossom explains as if that makes it all okay for two teen boys to be given weapons.

"That's not even the worst part." Aston starts, "When the teen girl learned they were offered a position for training, she threw a huge fit about misogyny in space and the strength of women until Rihu and Royi agreed to let her train as well."

"How old is the girl?" I ask, trying to remember her face from the pod.

"Demi Davidson will be thirteen in," Blossom pauses to calculate. "Sixteen days, twelve hours, and twenty-two minutes."

"What else?" I ask, strategizing in my head about how I can help our little team best.

"The last item of importance on the list is news of the *SS Herculean EP1*. The vessel was hit by an asteroid on its escape from the belt. It carried four women and eleven children, including the astrophysicist and aerospace engineer who worked on the project. They are now among the list of casualties with my sister Bubbles. This occurrence dropped your likelihood of a return to Earth from eight percent to two percent."

"Does that mean the other escape pods are still out there? That there is still a chance for them?"

"Yes, the other vessels still have a chance to return to earth or safety."

My heart aches as I realize that's now the best-case scenario. My mind races to find another answer as I watch Aston pace frenetically. If any of the escape pods could return to Earth, someone could come to save us here. If they could hold out for help, they would want to locate all the pods. Eventually, they would end up here. Ultimately, we would go home. *But how long until this became home?*

"People are dead!" Aston exclaims, "We are stuck here with kids of our own. Alba saw her husband's head roll in front of her and her baby girl. There is a baby who will never know her true parents. And you're in bed with one of the freaking aliens. We don't even know how friendly they are."

I take a deep breath before I say anything to Aston. As worried as I am about our little crew of people, Aston is finally speaking. She may be shouting her words at me and offending every alien within a thousand-foot radius, but she's talking. Her shock is gone, and it's finally sunk in. She's almost back to the best friend I know and love. I've been waiting impatiently for this moment. I'm happy it's here.

"Kano hasn't hurt me, taken advantage of me, or used me," I say, thinking of the night before. Even as I begged him to do the dirty with me, he turned me down. He clothed me and brought me somewhere safe, and we only slept. With his size, I would know if anything else had happened.

"The V`òllø are not considered a hostile race," Blossom adds, reminding Aston of what I've said.

"Well, one of the aliens has hurt me." She growls, crossing her arms over her chest.

It has been a while since I've seen this kind of fire in her eyes. The last time I remember her this worked up was when her father told her that an arts degree was for hippies and losers and that he wouldn't raise a hippy or a loser. She spent six weeks showing him how much dedication a degree in arts took over a degree considered more, 'logical.' It was a very intense time filled with many family debates over dinner, PowerPoint presentations, and one singular hand-to-hand combat between Aston and her brother. *Her brother she probably won't see again, thanks to you.*

"Who hurt you?" I'm surprised, to say the least. The aliens have been nothing but welcoming to me, even given my outburst last night.

"Llazho." She grumbles. The name tickles my brain, and I realize it's because that's one of the aliens who found their soulmates last night.

Like a lightbulb in the dark, I put it together.

"Llazho is your soulmate?" My voice is entirely too cheery for Aston's liking, and she makes that clear in the death glare I receive. She's smothered her sparkle so thoroughly that only embers remain, and all the flame has been directed at me. If looks could kill, am I right?

"Don't call him that. He's insufferable. Controlling. Domineering. He thinks he's always right. It's infuriating."

"Now I understand what this early morning visit is really about." I joke, even though my mind is still processing. There is no way I'm allowing the kids to handle weapons. And there is no way I will take our pitiful chance of getting home without fighting back. But Aston is finally talking to me, and it's about a guy. The moment is so human I can't help but stay in it.

"I don't even want to talk about him." She hisses. If Blossom can roll her eyes, I'm sure I saw it happen. The lavender light flashed in disbelief.

"Blossom, what do you know?" I ask, turning to the beautiful robotic woman.

"Llazho is a kind alien. He walked Aston home after you were flown here by the mount, Lewe. They spoke outside of things Aston has asked me to keep private."

"Aston," I say in reprimand, imagining dirty words.

"Only you would assume it was about that!" She smacks the air toward me in annoyance. "He just wanted to know why I was sitting next to Rihu, and I told him I didn't even know who Rihu was, and he didn't like that answer. He was all like, 'Rihu is a sky warrior. He is trouble.' And I was like, 'That's great, dude. Next time I'll sit between Kano and Vera' because I didn't want to be beside him in the first place. So, he got all grumpy with me and went into a freaking alien politics class about how sitting between *ĝhajo* is some alien form of swinging, and I told him it didn't matter, and he wouldn't freaking listen."

After her tirade, she gasps for a breath and looks out the wall of windows in Kano's bedroom. It reminds me of my loft, so I try not to look at it, but when Aston hooks onto something, I feel like I have to check it out.

It turns out to be her soulmate. Llazho has his horns locked in Kano's. He growls under his breath, and Kano gives him that smile he uses to tease me, and I wonder what's going on. Aston seems to think she knows what's happening as she storms out of the house toward Llazho.

"What is this?" she shouts, waving a hand at the display. I can see Kano detangle himself from the horn lock, and he shoots me a wink that sends heat to my belly. Aston's eyes are locked on Llazho's when she shouts, "First it's Rihu, and now Kano? You think you can fight because you have some ownership over me, buddy! That's not how human relationships work."

Llazho clearly enjoys this because he leans back and crosses his arms over his chest. One side of his mouth tilts up, and I can't wait to see where this goes, but Kano tugs me to his side. Then, looking down at me with moony eyes, he whispers, "It is a horn tangle. Should we tell your friend that it is friendly?"

I snort a laugh and shake my head. "Let's allow her to figure it out on her own."

That's how we end up together, watching as Llazho patiently lets her yell and rail at him. She talks all about the patriarchy and how even millions of lightyears from Earth, men are still alphaholes who think they have some kind of claim over her. He patiently listens, looking to Blossom for clarification but enjoying her tirade nonetheless. And when

Aston is finally finished, a full smile takes over Llazho's face. This surprises Kano beside me, and I can tell from the thing his eyes do. It surprises Aston too. So much she takes a step back and almost bumps into me.

"Aston, my little wildfire," He starts. I don't think he means it to be condescending from how his eyes sparkle back at hers, but I can see how it sounds to her human ears. "Do you know what it means when two V`òllø lock horns?"

"It's fighting. You looked like you were growling at him like you did at me last night!" She flings a hand toward Kano.

"Oh no, dear Aston. It is not like violence."

Her fire dies as she squeaks, "What?"

"It is like, how do you say? Human H-ugh."

Her eyes widen as she looks at Blossom. Blossom is quick to confirm. A rosy hue envelops her cheeks, and she looks mortified. Then, with a dignified foot stop and a harrumph, she twisted back towards Kano's room, and I tugged my way out of his arms to join her.

"Must you leave me, My Vera?" The way he asks makes my heart clench, but I nod. Aston was right when she stormed in this morning. We should do our best to update our two percent chance of escape. Until we've exhausted all the options, it's not fair to everyone for me to get too comfortable.

Kano's head falls almost imperceptibly, but he releases me. I flinch when I hear Aston shout my name, but I tear my eyes from his and join her again. We have a two percent chance of getting off this planet, and we have to take it.

CHAPTER NINETEEN

Llazho fumes when Az-ton moves away from him, and I can't help but grin at his displeasure. But my *jisa* is strong, and I can take his ire. So, I poke at his second heart as I walk toward the crystal fields to pray. He follows.

"It will be many moons before you win your *ĝha*."

He growls, "My heart already beats. She is already won. All that is left is for her to admit such."

"And that is the part you seem to struggle with," I joke, practically skipping across the chasm. Watching Vera go over the edge last night was terrifying, and I couldn't imagine what she was thinking. Why would she do such a silly thing? I push the energy away from my *jisa* and continue my walk-through town with Llazho.

Llazho does not do much praying. Where sometimes Royi or Zhu will join me for prayers in the first sliver of the sun, or the *peholoe* will join me at night, Llazho does not see the purpose. It revitalizes my *jisa*, comforts me, and helps me keep the faith. Llazho must not need those things, or perhaps he feels them when fishing. Still, he follows me all the way to the crystal fields today and kneels in their ashes with me. I pray under my breath, flicking my eyes toward him occasionally to see him do the same.

Together, we kneel and pray, and I can imagine we share a topic. Gratitude to the Baso Sheva for a *ĝha* and guidance on how to win their human hearts. A few of the younger males in our tribe join us, and when I am finished and stand, I realize the fields are full. The blessings of the Baso Sheva shine forth as the opportunity to earn a *ĝha* becomes a reality once again. My men pray for her favor.

It doesn't take long for the others to rise. The sun has risen to the next highest slice of the sky, and we all must do our part for the village. As some of the men pass by, we tangle horns, and they tell me their plans for the day. They invite me to meet them at the training grounds for the initiation of some humans or to join them on the farm. Unfortunately, I let them know their offers are appreciated, but I won't be able to make it today. Also, I have a matter of security to deal with.

Rihu and Royi catch up with me outside the fields, and we begin our mission together.

"How is our dearly *ĝha*-bound friend?" Rihu asks, bumping his shoulder against mine. I had a message sent to him last night to meet me after prayers with the first sliver of the sun. Human women were a blessing, but we did not know enough about them. It came to my attention that they were given a tour of Wupeso, but we were not invited into their spherical home. Since it came from the sky, we sky warriors were the ones who needed to investigate. Or at least that is what I told myself as I lay with my *ĝha* in my arms all night.

"I don't think you need to ask him," Royi touts. "I heard he was grinning like a fool all the way to prayers. I heard he got his *ĝha* to sleep in his bed with him."

Rihu's eye color widens slightly as he takes me in. It is true. My Vera stayed in my bed with me throughout the night. It is true. I loved every moment. But the way she acted earlier was unsettling. It did not mean much to her, and she tried to sneak away. Deceit she would not have admitted to if I hadn't caught her in the act, I'm sure. I found My Vera was very good at deception if she wanted to be. Before I could correct them of the night and the situation with my *ĝha*, we arrived at the human portal. I believe Blossom called it an escape pod. But if the Baso Sheva had a say in it, I imagine it's closer to a celestial delivery vessel.

"Wow. It seems even larger than before." Rihu says reverently. His closest friend squints at the top. It still floats on the water as the waves push it toward the bay's opening. The entrance still stands wide open.

My *jisa* flickers into place, and I keep my hand on my knife as I take my first steps into the odd ball. It smells floral and metallic – unnaturally clean. But underneath the smell of the pod, all the individual human scents tickle my nose. Particularly that of my *ĝha*. I follow the scent of her to where she must have slept before. The bed is much smaller than mine, with another equally small bed stacked atop it with barely enough space for a human to sit up. But, unlike the other beds, my Vera's is decorated neatly. A small pad lies at the top, tucked partially under her sheets.

Connecting with the Baso Sheva, I open my third eye to inspect the room further. It shines like crystal fields. Dozens of colors blend and fray around the surfaces of the room. The energy seems to bounce off the walls and grow in the center of the room. But what attracts me most is the energy of My Vera. Her bedding drips in her soul essence, mixed with one of red.

I kneel beside it in reverence, wondering how many days she spent here. From the few facts I gathered at the welcome dinner, they spent much time among the stars on a much larger vessel before they had to escape some evil beasts. None of that came from my *ĝha*'s lips, though. Hers were pinched closed as she listened to the people around her, reading their faces like scripture. I close my third eye.

This is something I realized about my *ĝha*. She liked to study. Her surroundings, her people, my people. She picked up on many of our customs quickly by watching quietly. It's not that she has spent a lot of time here, but that she is attuned to the behaviors of beings. That is why it is so confusing that she was not cautious in her departure last night. She had been studying me thoroughly enough to see my announcement, yet she ran with abandon. I grumble, smacking the pad of fluff angrily. A feather as white as snow puffs out, and I pull an item from beneath her sheets, finding a little box with unfamiliar patterns displayed on the front. Sharp, human letters are displayed at the top, and at this moment, I wished I understood her language better.

I hold them close to my face to inspect them, and I can't help but think it still smells like her. A smokier, darker version of my Vera. It makes me think of the version of Vera that tries to deceive me. I returned to the task, tucking away the strange box for later.

Together, Rihu, Royi, and I search the pod for clues about the humans, but the things we find confuse us further. There are clothes and beds much like ours, but then there are these indescribable things like sunlight they've embedded in their sleeping cubbies and a contraption with latches and circles that make pushing it along easier. We investigate the vessel and learn that the Baso Sheva has sent us more than females. She has sent us tools and knowledge. Human ingenuity.

"I wish Blossom were here to explain this mess," Royi says, and a low drone begins before Blossom's artificial voice titters through the chamber.

"Kano and friends, how may I help you?"

Rihu snaps around the room, looking for our metallic pink friend, but she is nowhere in sight. The low buzz of white noise sounds from above, and when I look up, she is not there.

"Where are you, Blossom?"

"My full body is on a walk with Miss Vera Oksana and Aston Andrews. My ship device functions separately from my body."

"This is a ship?" Rihu asks.

"Yes. This is an escape pod for the *SS Herculean*." Her voice replies.

"Can you see me?" Royi asks, doing an awkward jump in the air.

"Yes."

"What can you tell us about the humans?" I ask, "And these items?"

"I have already introduced the roster of women, but if you want to know about age, occupation, and dietary preferences, I have those on file."

"Yes." I practically shouted, "What did My Vera do in the human world?"

"Vera Oksana is a professional gambler," Blossom responds. I have never heard this word, but it translates as a talented game player.

"Humans play games to support the tribe?"

"No. Humans play games in many capacities. Vera played games to earn money."

Money also has no direct translation, and it sounds ludicrous. A form of currency to generalize trade. Before I can ask more questions, my men step in.

"What about Az-ton?" Rihu asks.

"And Daria?" Royi puts in.

Blossom doesn't hesitate to answer, "Aston Andrews was an heiress to a large group of hotels," daughter of a man who owned many temporary homes for large groups of people, "and a gallerist," someone who sells art.

"Daria Davidson was a nurse." Healer.

This news about the woman Daria makes Royi's *jisa* flash in excitement. The color of his eyes explodes, "She is a healer. I must go to her at once, introduce her to —

"Royi, we are working," Rihu says, clapping his closest friend on the back. "We cannot abandon Kano to go chase after the new women."

But I have more questions, so I dismiss them. When they are finally gone, I sit cross-legged at the center of the chamber and ask, "What game did My Vera play on Earth? Can you teach me?"

CHAPTER TWENTY

After an hour of primping and priming, Aston finally allows us to leave Kano's swiftly warming hut. We are barely two steps outside when one of the older alien women approaches us.

"Veh-ruh. Veh-ruh." The woman calls, practically stumbling over herself to get to us. She's much smaller than Kano but still significantly taller than me. She looks like she's built to play linebacker, but her face shows she doesn't have an angry bone in her body. She tries to smile, and her skin does that strange shimmer like the others. When she reaches us, Aston smiles politely in her direction before trying to step around her. The woman steps to the side, blocking our path though she maintains her face of pleasantness. We try to dance around her again, but she steps into our way again.

"Can we help you?" Aston asks. Her friendliness wanes. She wants to get off this planet because her family is on Earth. She also wants to get off this planet thanks to a specific alien man she avoids. Still, Blossom translates for the woman, and she tilts her head from side to side.

"Veh-ruh can." She touts, pointing her horns in my direction. I jump back from their points when she comes towards me with them.

"Whoa. We can talk. There's no need to tangle," I cry, taking another step away.

The woman looks confused and rejected. If an alien can look confused and rejected, that is. She points her horns at me again, and I look at Blossom in panic. I know it's friendly, but I don't know how to respond here.

"It's called a tangle," Blossom explains. "She wants to tangle her horns with yours. Like Kano and Llazho did this morning. A way to show trust and have a positive chemical reaction."

"I know, but I still don't have horns," I point out.

"Just touch them with your hands," Aston whispers, glancing behind her. The man she argued with earlier is on the bay, glaring at us. I grab ahold of the woman's horns for a moment, and when she stands straight once again, she tries for another smile. Blossom translates.

"I'm Zhalisee. I heal for the tribe." She says, and I can hear the pride in her words. "You are Veh-ruh, and you are *Ĝha* of Kano. He is a good man."

"He is." I agree skeptically, trying to skirt around the woman. She steps in our path once again.

"You don't understand," Blossom translates for her. "Kano is not only a good man. He is the *best* man. He had faith for you even when the *peholoe* stopped believing."

Her words make me want to squirm, but I leave the wriggling unease inside. This woman didn't have to tell me about Kano being the best man. Last night, I was in Kano's bed, high off a sex drug, and he didn't pressure me. In fact, he refused to 'tangle' until I was better. Kano took all of us weird human creatures into his village. He held a welcome dinner. He ensured we had the nicest accommodations available, even though Roxie intended to shoot them upon arrival, and Aston thought they would eat us. In less than twenty-four hours – does this planet do twenty-four-hour days? – he's proven himself to be better than many Earthmen. The kind healer didn't need to vouch for him with me because it made no difference.

We were still human. We still weren't meant to be here. And I had to do everything in my power to get my team back to earth.

"I'm sure Kano would appreciate your praise," I say, trying for diplomacy. Then, I try to step around her, and she steps in our way once again. Aston groans beside me, and I realize her *ĝha* is moving in.

"He does not need it." Zhalisee huffs, clearly frustrated with my misunderstanding.

"Zhalisee," I start, tripping over my tongue with the soft j sound in her name, "You clearly want to help me, as Kano's *ĝha*, to understand what he's like. And Aston and I want to understand more about your village. So maybe you can show us the lay of the land, and we can chat more about Kano?"

"The land lies flat. The islands fly." She says, confusion coloring her expression.

Aston has moved closer to my back, and I can tell we're en route to disaster if she is forced to deal with her own *ĝha* anytime soon.

"Right; I mean, I'd like to meet Kano's people so I can better understand him." I hope my words appeal to her motivations, and they must because she bows her horns to me and leads us away.

Meeting the people of Wupeso was a colossal mistake. I thought Zhalisee's insistence on Kano and I being together was bad this morning, but it was only the beginning. I told the woman I wanted to go to the training grounds, and she took her sweet time getting us there, stopping in numerous places along the way. We stopped at the home of a clothier, who insisted on taking my measurements with a fibrous string. All the while, she chatted on and on about Kano and how strong he was. She spouted about changing his shirts to fit over his muscles or something shallow like that. I hadn't cared about the musculature of a man since I turned thirty. And I told her I didn't care about Kano's either, but she called my bluff.

When her husband came in with the remnants of butchered animals down the front of his apron, he told me how Kano supported his ranch by negotiating on his behalf with their nearest neighbor to bring a better variety of animals to their village. Then, Zhalisee introduced us to her healing protegee, who told me that if I were to have Kano's babies, he could make labor much more manageable. His innate specialty had to do with babies, and until we had arrived, the protegee did not know the purpose of his gift. He only helped Zhalisee birth one child in the last few years.

Finally, we reached the training grounds, and it only got worse. I expected to see three young children, strapped into metal armor with terrible swords, fighting. I expected a missing limb and blood all over the battlefield with how long it took us to arrive. Instead, one of the warriors sat cross-legged, leading the three children through prayers meant for stilling the mind; three other warriors sat behind them, doing the same. Upon arrival, another warrior met us at the gate to give us a safety speech. He talked about how we will not be allowed to touch the weapons without one of them present and how we should stick with our guide as we tour the space. My relief for the children was overwhelming.

The problem was that the warriors had nothing but good things to say about Kano and their planet. Kano is caring. Kano is kind. Kano is faithful. Kano is loyal. On and on they went telling me about how great of a man Kano was and how silly it would be for me to reject the bond I had with him, which I didn't even know was an option until that moment. Rihu was the one to let it spill, and Royi had smacked the side of his horn for saying it.

Worse yet, none of them believed me when I said I appreciated their words, but I didn't feel that way about Kano. I explained that I believed them, but we weren't bonded in this mystical way they all thought we were.

The whole day was very enlightening, to say the least, but not in the way I would have hoped. A two-percent chance of escaping this planet was better than nothing, and Aston was unhappy, two major points in the leaving Kano category. They sat in line with other reasons like Kano is an alien, and I just met Kano, and he already thinks of me as his. Then, there were the reasons that made me want to stay. I had nothing to return to; my career was over, most of my family was dead, and the ones that weren't didn't like me since I stopped sending money. Kano is everything his people have said he is, and I love the concept of a soulmate. Moreover, I began to love Wupeso thanks to the day's activities and the fantastic people.

The clothier had taken my measurements and promised to deliver some clothes in the coming days. The healer heard about Aston's trouble sleeping and offered her a tonic. The warriors all reassured me that they would take good care of the children and that none of them would see a blade until they came of age in human terms. Yes, they also spoke of how amazing Kano was, but they seemed genuinely pleased to meet me, Aston, and Blossom. They did not treat us differently for looking different, and they all banded together to ensure we had what we needed.

In all the ways that mattered, I learned Wupeso was nothing like Earth. It was better.

CHAPTER TWENTY-ONE

Kano finds me eating dinner with Aston, Blossom, Zhalisee, and one of the local families. Supposedly in the warmer seasons, it is usual to eat outside of the home in Wupeso. So, we're all gathered around a low table, sitting in the mossy grass, overlooking the bay as the sun sets across the water. Zhalisee has introduced me to a drink they call *tsare,* which is a lot like bubbly wine, and I'm on my third glass when I feel a tug in my chest.

My first thought is that it's a symptom of an impending heart attack, and then I hear Kano's smooth, deep voice and Blossom's chirpy translation.

"May I join you? I find the view is spectacular here."

My skin prickles at the rumbling sound of his voice. With every step he takes closer to me, it's like I can feel the cells of my body reaching out to him. It's eerie and concerning, and I wonder what kind of magnetic field the guy is made of to attract me. No. Not attract because we aren't attracted to random alien men on random distant planets. I turn to greet him, and my eyes meet the fabric of his shirt.

It's white and woven like the kind rich men used to wear when I would strip on their yacht. As my eyes scrape up his chest, I realize it ties in the front like a pirate shirt, and there's a collar to keep the dust off his deep green skin. I force myself to tear my eyes away. It takes me a second, and I have to crane my neck, but eventually, my eyes reach his. He said the view was beautiful, but I felt he spoke about me. If it were anyone else, I would have gagged.

"Kano," I say. It's meant to be a greeting, but the way his mouth tilts makes it seem like so much more than that.

"Vera." He replies, inching a little closer. His leg brushes my shoulder, and I jump a little at the current of unexpected buzzing that washes through me. Aston clears her throat, and I tear my eyes away, feeling the flush on my cheeks. I scramble to scoot over and make space for him at the tiny table, but Zhalisee doesn't move at all, focusing instead on the meal in front of her. I send a pleading look to Aston on my other side, and she grumbles under her breath before sliding down the table closer to Blossom.

Next thing I know, Kano's entire leg brushes against mine, and our kind hosts offer him food and beverages like he's the freaking King. A zing of shock runs through me when I realize he *is* the King. He's their chief, their leader. They all love him and praise him because he cares for them and their interests. Everyone in this town, all day long, spoke of him in such high regard because he's not like an earth leader. No, he's loyal and kind, and helpful. He listens to his people and leads them with the faith that things will work out for them. Then, they do. Everything comes up Kano.

I finish my fourth glass of tsare and try to catch my breath. Kano fills my glass once again, and I stop my whimper at my lips. If he's King, that will make me Queen. Or something akin to it. All these people would rely on me and have expectations of me. They would want me to symbolize faith like Kano does regularly. I down my glass. He offers to pour me another, and I shake my head, scooting away from the table and standing in the grass.

I'm not an expert in foreign expressions, but I can see confusion from a mile away, especially on Kano's face. It's like he can't keep any thoughts from me. *And me anything from him.* I must look like a deer in the headlights as my head swivels, trying to find an escape route. The people we eat with are lovely, but their outdoor dining area is fenced in and thatched to keep out the wind. There's a gate, but the latch looks complicated, and honestly, I'm not in the mood to find

104

out exactly how wrong I might be about the mechanism. Then, there's the door to their hut, but my human upbringing tells me that would be equally as rude an exit. Which leaves me only one choice.

The fence is only five feet, and I didn't get kicked out of my family for nothing. I take three bounding steps toward the fence and jump. Then, like I'm a teenage girl, rather than a possible alien queen, I hop the fence and run. Well, it's more like I jump the fence and disappear. I crouch along the wall and skirt through the village until I find the street. Then, I duck beside a building and think.

Thanks to where we ate, I had options for escape. The karst is around the corner, but many women and children have spent all day there, and I likely wouldn't get the chance to be alone. I need the space. Past that, there are the crystal fields everyone has told me about, but Kano is known to frequent those. So, it's a risk. Finally, we were overlooking the bay, so if I followed one of the winding trails through the tall grass, I could find myself on a beach. But then, I remember the mushroom incident and decide I don't want any alien plant life rubbing up on me without Blossom telling me it's safe.

Crystal fields it is.

I stay close to the buildings as I steal along the path, ducking out of the way whenever I hear the breathy alien speech. It makes the hike up the hill slow-going but gives me plenty of time to be alone with my thoughts. All of which are catastrophic in nature.

It starts with guilt over ditching Aston with Zhalisee and Kano. Sure, Aston also has Blossom, but the AI woman didn't think the same way humans did. Her emotions were more binary and controllable. She knew her purpose and didn't have human weaknesses to fret over. So, Aston's big emotions about dating aliens, being stranded so far from family, and having her future taken from her could only be connected with so much. On the other hand, Blossom was pretty upset about her sister's escape pod, so maybe Aston would be fine.

Then, it went to my shame around my behavior. On the ship, I was commanding. I kept my emotions close to the vest and led the women. They listened to me because they needed direction in the absolute chaos of the ship's crash and subsequent invasion. They needed leadership in the pod to cope with the worsening situation. They required a softer touch than Roxie, who was ready to solve the problem with the rounds in her chamber if it came to that. I shudder.

I make it to the top of the hill, huffing breath. I'm not sure whether it's from my anxiety or the hike. Then, a warm breeze presses the unfamiliar fabrics against my sweat-slicked skin, bringing a fresh, familiar smell with it. I take a deep breath, close my eyes, and tilt my head toward the sky. As I breathe out, I bring my face forward and open my eyes.

"Wow," I breathe, taking it all in. The crystals are embedded in soft, shimmering purple sand that glints off the planet's rays of sunlight. Varied shades of red and blue glitter with an intense inner light, creating rainbow fractals in the sand. As I walk along the path, further into the field, I see some crystals barely the size of my fingernail. The sand shifts around them like shells. Then, there are others that tower over me like monolithic spires, shading me in their intense color.

Heat radiates from my left, and I turn toward the red crystal structure. Jagged, curling pieces twist and twine around each other, creating an archway of warm heat. Walking beyond the archway, I find an open space in the sand where the blue crystals have grown and spread along the ground like morning glory on a vine. Some take on the unique patterns of snowflakes, and others have the veiny look of human flowers. Here, sprouts of a pink coral-like plant grow and fray into their own wild designs. Their porous skin seems to breathe in the passing breeze. Somehow, I understand how they feel.

The path turns under another archway, and I follow it deeper into the space. My shoes collapse into the sand beneath my feet, and I lean against a cool blue crystal spire to take them off. Then, the sand crinkles between my toes. I don't know how long I will follow the path, but a V`òllø voice sounds like whispers echoing around me when I reach the end and find one of the *peholoe* kneeling before a totem of blue and red crystals that have grown together into a gigantic purple mass. A lavender mist is held in the cavernous space beneath it, and a line of woven mats sit before it.

From where I stand, I can tell the *peholoe* whispers in prayer. I think it is Gowi, but I cannot tell. Their horns are bowed, their words are reverent, and they echo through the space. It feels haunting and ethereal. And it draws me in and encourages me to try my hand.

I don't interrupt the *peholoe*, but I follow their lead. Finding a mat beside them, I kneel on it and bow my head. The woven wood bends beneath my weight, and I let my eyes flutter closed, trying to think of the words I wish to say. The immediate feeling of imposter syndrome wipes over me in waves, and I'm reminded of the last time I prayed on my knees.

I was fifteen years old, and I had lost my virginity. My period was a week late. I'd peed on a pregnancy stick I bought from the dollar store because I couldn't afford more, and it looked similar enough to my sister's drug tests that no one would ask any questions if they paid enough attention to my trash. I was supposed to wait ten minutes, and the whole time I knelt on the bathroom rug with my head bowed and my arms folded and resting across the tub's cool edge. I prayed. I begged God to send me my period and promise I wasn't pregnant. I begged him to keep me from becoming like my mother because, unlike her, I wouldn't get the loveless marriage and the financial help.

The father of this possible child wasn't like my dad. No, he was six years older than me, in his first year of college. My friends had convinced me to use a fake ID and go out partying at this local bar. He took my V-card in the bathroom as he pressed me against the back of an occupied stall. I didn't tell him no or stop. I couldn't even think with his beer breath in my ear, cascading across my face and neck. After the sharp sting of his first thrust, I had no chance of vocalizing anything. And I didn't blame him because, truthfully, I didn't know what the encounter had meant until later – when I was sitting alone in a bathroom stressing about my period.

That day I prayed, and God didn't answer. The stick said I was pregnant, and I couldn't even remember the father's name. I confirmed it at a free clinic and told them there was no way I could have an abortion. I wouldn't be able to live with my own guilt. It turned out it didn't matter. I knew God had forsaken me for good when I miscarried alone in my bathroom two months later.

I bled painfully for days. And there was an emotional loss no one could understand or prepare me for. Worse, no one knew about it.

The breeze whistles through a slot in a crystal and snaps me out of my reverie. Salty tears drip from my eyes, gathering little balls of darkened, wet sand beside my prayer mat. An unjust mix of fear, grief, and rage rips at me. I sob into my hands. I can't remember the last time I cried or screamed, or pitched a fit. It had to be before I started playing poker and probably even before that. Sure, there had been brief brushes of sadness, a wayward tear at a heart-wrenching movie, or a watery eye from the rage of losing a game. But nothing like this.

I collapse in on myself and sob into the little cocoon I've wrapped myself in. My tears are like an unstoppable wave. I'm vaguely aware of the scene I'm causing, but I couldn't pull it together if I tried. My life on earth was a series of unfortunate events. Teen parents with no education raised my sister and me with no money or help. My sister's addiction made her so ill it was hard to look at her face. My friends thought doing illicit activities on the weekend was cool and congratulated me for sleeping with that guy. Then, there was the pregnancy. The miscarriage. My mother kicked me out because I stopped lending my sister money for drugs. My father refused to pick up my calls. I stripped in seedy places for years before dragging myself out of the gutter to strip in nicer establishments. Dancing for men who thought the word no meant a higher price tag. Then, ultimately, doing something for myself. Poker. It was my peace, and emotions had no place. I was good at playing. I made my money. I retired. I lived my dream, in retirement, by myself. I'd sent my sister to rehab. She finished rehab in the summer, and she was coming to visit. We were going to reconnect.

But I pushed my luck. I saw tickets to space, and I thought, go for it. I would win them, and then the changes I'd undergone would be out of this world. Of course not. No, that was pure ego to think I could visit space and come home. That wasn't how my life worked. It wasn't how things went for Vera Oksana. Obviously, I dragged Aston – the only blessing to keep my life worth living – into my mess with me, and now she might never get home.

No matter how hard I try to muffle them, my sobs echo and sing through the field of crystals. I'm sure the *peholoe* beside me must think I'm crazy. I bet V`òllø don't even cry. I bet they're sitting there wondering what is going on with me. If I'm exploding or if it's some human custom. The thought is so crazy I laugh. And then, I'm cackling. I roll onto my butt in the sand, letting the tears fall and laughing. The salty taste of my crying hits my tongue, and I can't even find it in myself to care because, of course, I ended up on an alien planet. Of course, I'm supposed to be some alien queen. Of course, some poor, unsuspecting alien elder would be privy to my biggest meltdown in years.

When my cackling dies down, and I can see through my tears, I look over and realize the *peholoe* is gone. I didn't know when they left, but a part of me had the decency to feel bad about scaring them off with my hysterics.

I don't bother kneeling again when I finally start to pray. Instead, I cross my legs and lean forward to gather purple sand in my hands. I let it glide through my fingertips as I speak.

"God, or whatever higher power sent me here, I want you to know this is not a hilarious joke. I don't find it charming or funny. Two percent? Two percent! Ha." I've really lost it now.

"You know what's really funny?" I ask no one in particular – since no one is here.

"What's really funny is that you think this would phase me. What is actually hilarious is that you think putting me in front of a hot dude who wants nothing but to please me is a punishment! It's so funny, in fact, that I might go for it. The only time I succeeded in something was when I was a selfish heathen. When my whole family rebuked me for making money in such a sketchy way. Why couldn't I fall in love the same way? Huh?"

My voice echoes, silence falls, and some of my fire dims. No response from God comes floating down in a gigantic silver spacecraft, that's for sure. I wait a few moments longer to see if anything will happen, but it doesn't. So, I stand from the sand and brush the crystalline granules from my skirts. When I turn

around, Kano stands there, the jade color of his eyes like
pinpricks trained on me.

CHAPTER TWENTY-TWO

Kano

My *Ĝha*'s eyes are puffy and red, but otherwise, she looks fine. She spoke softly in her staggering language as she sifted crystal shards through her fingertips. Upon arrival, a sharp 'Ha' escaped her, and I wondered if she spoke with the Baso Sheva about our bond. I'm surprised to find her so calm now. When Gowi came running from the crystal fields talking nonsense about my *Ĝha* experiencing some terrible illness, I was concerned, to say the least. This was nothing like my expectations.

No, My Vera is perfectly whole. The rim of pain around her eyes is the only hint of something wrong. She did not have these when she left the dinner table.

Her hands freeze on her thighs when she notices I'm here, and her little eye circles roll around in their sockets at the sight of me. I don't know what this means, but I hope it is good. Blossom could not accompany me into the sand, she tried to explain her concern about it affecting something inside her, but it felt like information for one's *ĝha*, not me. So, instead, she provided me with one of the tiny ear-beans that work the same as her translation capabilities. Blossom had already scrapped them from the ship and given them to the human women.

"Of course, you're here," She says in choppy human words. I put the word bean inside my ear, and Blossom's voice chirps, a trilling noise that doesn't translate.

I offer her my hand. She stares at it, placing her hands on her hips, before storming back down the path. Her human feet are bare, slipping and sliding beneath the crystal shards and flicking them up behind her minimally.

"Blossom says these ear-beans will translate," I tell her, catching up to walk by her side. It's selfish of me to stand beside her when I know my place is watching her back. Keeping her safe. But I can protect her from any angle, and I love watching her face when she speaks. It bunches, smooths, and shifts with her moods and tells me so much about her thoughts.

"Ear-beans?" She asks, her brows scrunching in that way that tells me her displeasure. "Do you mean earbuds?"

"Yes," I say, my grin grows. I knew My Vera would know the odd words of Blossom. But, even better, the earbuds work.

"Great, well," She pulls hers out of her ear and shoves it in my hand, "I don't want to talk."

I dip my horns in understanding and hold the bud firmly in my hand. We walk silently, and I relax into the crystal fields' energy. Since the crystals create sharp sand, many small creatures avoid burrowing in it. Because of their heat and cold, the larger animals also avoid them. It makes the crystal fields one of the safest places in Wupeso, which is one reason why we consider it sacred.

Even though I did not come to pray, I can already feel my stressors melting away. We pass a patch of *tziruga,* and I notice my Vera trailing a finger over the vine. Her hand snaps back when she realizes how cold they are to the touch. The petals are crystalline and maintain that coolness for many moons after they are plucked, but when the light inside them dies, they crumble. It helps us store our food, and I want to tell her, but when I try to offer the bud, she refuses it again.

When we finally reach the bottom of the karst, she turns toward the stairs, and my hearts feel like they are rending from my chest.

"I'm going to bed, Kano. I'll talk to you tomorrow."

My heart sinks as I watch her turn toward the stairs. She has never seemed so defeated as she does now, and I worry about what it will do to My Vera if I let her go like this. I don't want to let her go.

"Wait," I say, knowing she can't understand me. Still, she stops on the stairs and turns to look at me expectantly. I offer her the earbud. A shiver works through my *jisa* at the brush of her hand against mine. I watch as she puts it in her tiny ear – smaller and rounder than mine. I pull the cards from a pouch on my trousers, "Can we play a game?"

CHAPTER TWENTY-THREE

"*Not the cards!*" *Aston whines, stomping her foot like the heiress she is. I ignore her outburst, tucking them into the pocket of my jeans. I haven't gone anywhere without them since I won that game. The dealer was confused when I asked to keep them. They had already been marked for disuse.*

"They're good luck." I spout, slipping my belt through the loops of my jeans.

"You don't need luck." Aston smiles, "You have me."

"Where did you get those?" I asked, snatching the box out of his hand. I thought I had lost them in the tunnel of *SS Herculean.* They weren't on my person when I helped Alba, so I figured I'd dropped them in the rush. It had crushed me when I reached for them and didn't find them in my back pocket as usual. I opened the box, and aside from a tiny dent in the left corner and the slices from discontinuation, they were perfectly intact. I'm momentarily full of gratitude.

"I found them on the *ship,*" Kano says, sheepishly rubbing the tops of his horns.

"You went to the escape pod? When?" I ask, stepping closer to him. I'm about four steps above him and still have to look up at him. His height is ridiculous.

"With the peak of the sun. The pod came from the sky. It is the responsibility of the sky warriors." He explains. I notice his eyes flash from full color to an absence of it and back. Then, he presses forward, "Blossom said —"

"Blossom was with me all morning." I interrupt, putting my free hand on a hip.

"*Ship* Blossom." He explains, "The *ship* Blossom explained that this is for a game called *poker*. A game you played in your home world."

I rub my thumb over the raised embossing of the casino logo, and relief shudders through me. I don't know what he means by Ship Blossom, but having my lucky cards in hand calms me. I didn't realize how attached I had been to my cards until they appeared. No, until Kano returned them to me because he knew they would be important to me. Looking up at Kano, I can see the hopefulness in his features that I will teach him how to play, and I really badly want to. So, I can feel them in my hands again. I stay silent for a few more moments, searching his face. I can tell he's hardly breathing, waiting for me to tell him about poker, but I don't.

Instead, I say, "Well, would you like to try a hand?"

CHAPTER TWENTY-FOUR

I did not know what my *ĝha* meant by "try a hand." I had already tried hands. I had two of my own, and they worked great for various uses, from working to hunting to holding my *ĝha*. But then, My Vera grabbed one of my hands and tugged me up the stairs of the karst. She dragged me along to the *peholoe*'s – now the human women's – home and into the main living room, where she sat me down and explained the rules.

"We're playing Texas Hold 'Em." She explains, pulling the flat, thin wafers of plant fibers out of the container. I watch in fascination as her hands maneuver the flat pieces into different places within the pile. She calls them cards. There are runes, shapes, and characters on one side and decorative art on the other. The characters turn out to be human numbers, and there are four shapes that are something she calls suits. The rules feel complicated, but she promises we will play a practice 'round.'

She shows me two cards and talks about wagers and how they work. The cards feel smooth and waxy, reminding me of the Alohkab'uli plant. There are arbitrary rules for what cards are good and what cards are great, and we make our bets based on what we intuit our odds to be without letting our opponent know our intentions. Or at least, that is how I understand the rules.

By the time we started our practice round, many other human women had gathered around to watch. The woman, Az-ton, who I have determined is my *ĝha*'s closest friend, sits behind me while the woman Alba bounces the babe gently in her arms to my side. Across from me, all I see is my *ĝha*. Her beautiful hair falls long across her chest, standing out from the brighter color of her dress. But the human women don't flock to her because of her beauty. They flock to her because she leads them. She assures them they will be okay and helps them adjust. They sit beside her because it is somewhere they feel safe. A feeling of warmth blooms in my hearts, making them beat more fervently.

"Do your people have *money? Currency?*" My *ĝha* asks, peeking across the cards she has laid on the mat in front of us.

These words do not make sense even with translation. They did not on the *ship* either. According to Blossom's translation, money is a plant fiber used in exchange for a good or service. Goods and services belong to the community in Wupeso. Everyone provides what they are best at and receives what they need. Except for the *peholoe*, who are blessed by the Baso Sheva and provide only wisdom. My face must look relatively blank because my *ĝha* tries a different approach to her wagers.

"Okay, so no currency. What do you value?" She asks. I don't get the chance to answer because her friend, Az-ton, snorts.

"*Ĝhajo*. Mates." Az-ton circles her eyes, but My Vera's eyes light up.

"Perfect. This round, we will play for a kiss." She announces, much to the surprise of the group. And myself. I would very much like to tangle lips with my *ĝha*.

Vera continues, "You can wager anything in poker. It's how I ended up here. Had I thrown that game, maybe you would have been sitting next to Mr. Big Money instead."

I don't know what she means about Mr. Big Money, but I tilt my horns to the side in agreement anyway. She flips over the first cards and peeks at her hand. I look at my own cards and back at Az-ton behind me. The pointy arrow-like cards are good if there is more than one or the face cards, so I say I will

118

raise our bet. She matches my bet, and we continue with the next round.

I don't quite understand why My Vera likes this game, but I can feel the excitement coming off of her. It makes my *jisa* shift with pleasure. So we go on this way, putting more and more kisses on the line until it is finally time to reveal our cards.

I flip mine over with no expectations since it is my first game. Still, Baso Sheva smiles down at me.

"You won." My *ĝha* says, mouth agape. I wonder if this is a preparation for a kiss and open my own mouth. Then, her eyes flick to mine, and I realize that was not true. She was surprised by my victory. She did not expect me to win, but I am a fierce warrior. Even in games, I oft win. It is my biggest strength, having The Baso Sheva on my side.

"Now, we kiss," I say, my own excitement coming through.

"It was a practice round," Vera says, her cheeks heating. She stares at the cards before us, then glances behind me at Az-ton. Az-ton plucks the cards up from in front of us and begins shuffling.

"She's right, Kano. You can't play a real round without a dealer. So, I'll deal this time. No more practice." Az-ton gives my *ĝha* a look I don't understand. Vera shakes off her loss, rolling back her shoulders.

I finally understand what this practice round meant. The energy in the room seems to shift, becoming heavier on my horns. I drop my head toward the floor and watch as Az-ton deals the cards to their proper locations. I grin at My Vera, and she does not smile back. Instead, her face drops into a mask of indifference as she stares back at me. She looks at her cards, and I look for an inkling of what she might be feeling or thinking, but it does not change. Her heart rate doesn't pick up, her nose doesn't twitch, and she doesn't change her grip on the cards. There is absolutely nothing on her face but indifference.

I think my cards are reasonable, so I told My Vera I would like to raise the bet. She matches it, and more cards are revealed. I look over to Alba to confirm my cards are good, but she ignores my hand and focuses on the youngling. So, I raise the bet again.

"Double the kisses."

My Vera matches my bet once again. We come to our last round of wagers, and my *ĝha* looks up at me from beneath her lashes. Still, I cannot see her usual expressions on her face. Instead, she glances at her cards, the house, and then back at me.

"I'd like to make a deal," she tells me, her voice confident and sure.

"What would be the conditions of this deal?" I ask, casually resting my cards face-down in front of me.

"If you win this hand, I will stay in Wupeso and be your mate, your *ĝha*. Like you hoped. If I win, you must help us human women get home to Earth."

My hearts stutter in my chest. The other women's eyes snap to my *ĝha*, but she looks at me. No, she looks through me. As far as I understand, my cards are great, but neither of us knows what the final card should be. I have as much chance of losing my kisses as I do of winning them, and my *ĝha* wants to raise this bet in the most valuable way.

I'm not the kind of man to risk it all on a game. Not usually, but if I fold, how will my *ĝha* look at me? I look at my cards once again, my *jisa* tense around me. Then, I nod my agreement.

120

"If you win, I will help you leave me." The cards are revealed, and the moment feels suspended in time.

CHAPTER TWENTY-FIVE

I lost. *I'm lost.* A hollow ache spreads through my chest, and my mouth parts in disbelief. It's like a car wreck on the side of the freeway; I can't stop looking. It's like I've slowed down to witness the most humbling moments in humanity. There's no anger. No depression. Only disbelief, loss, grief.

"The chances of returning to Earth without leadership are lower than before," Blossom announces as I stare at the cards.

Kano placed down a royal flush, a near-impossible hand. My eyes can't compute the two cards in front of him. I try to find any way my cards could beat his, but they're worse. I lost. After a three-year winning streak, I lost the highest-stake game I had ever played. I want to be angry, but I can't. I suggested the deal. I trusted my hand. I overlooked his casual tone when we discussed the deal.

"I guess beginner's luck is a universal law." Roxie jokes. I'm still frozen in place. I overlooked beginners' luck. I agreed to be his mate. I agreed to stay here. I gave up my life. Willingly! Over a game I never lose. My breath becomes sharp and shallow. It hurts to drag it into my lungs. Black spots flash around the edges of my vision, and I gasp.

Then, Kano is by my side, pulling me into his lap. I didn't realize how cold I was until I could feel the warmth of his body press in around me like a favorite blanket. With one big hand, he pulls my hair away from my neck, and with the other, he hugs me around my waist. His voice is at my ear when he orders, "Breathe."

I drag my breath into my lungs and expect the same sharp pain as before, but I'm met with fresh, warm air. Kano rubs his thumb over my lower belly soothingly, letting me come apart in his arms. I take another breath and remember what I've done. I stay in Kano's lap as I survey the women of the room. Aston speaks with Blossom in hushed tones, her eyes darting between the massive alien who calms me down with a simple touch and me. Alba holds the sleeping baby, who is pure and unaware of the trauma everyone is experiencing. Except for Roxie, she looks happy. She's smiling, undisturbed by the terrible news Blossom spouted off.

They had a two percent chance of getting home, and I made that lower, but none of them seemed mad.

"I, for one, am happy you lost," Roxie announces, pulling a glare from Alba. Aston gives a sharp shake of her head at Roxie, but the woman doesn't care. Instead, she rolls her eyes and carries on, "Earth is awful. Wupeso is awesome. Earlier today, one of the *peholoe* taught me to bake sweet rolls from some leaves that taste like cinnamon sugar toast, and she didn't even charge me for it. Last night, while you were God knows where doing God knows what, one of the warrior dudes asked me a thousand questions about my gun, and I got to teach him about automatic rifles. This place rocks."

"Roxie!" Alba reprimands, even though there is no bite to her words. She looks tired but not angry.

"Oh, come on, Alba. You feel the same way I do. Tell Vera about your situation. She obviously feels like crap for abandoning us to the scary locals. Make her feel better about it."

Alba sighs profoundly, and we all wait for her to respond. Even Kano leans in behind me, pressing his chest closer to my back to listen. I hate that I like it.

"Let's say my husband was not the calm, charismatic man everyone believed him to be. If I were to return to Earth after what happened on the ship, I could not guarantee my own safety."

Roxie mouths, "Mafia," at me.

Their words soothe me slightly, but I still can't kick my guilt. I turn my eyes to Aston. I know she has family at home, and I know she loves them. She's the one I wanted to go home for. She's the one who deserves the opportunity to return to Earth. Roxie and Alba follow my eyes to Aston, and I watch their unspoken words hit their target.

"Ugh! Fine," Aston grumbles, stomping her foot. "I don't want to go back either."

My eyes widen in shock. My mouth gapes. This is not what I expected from my best friend. Aston Andrews loves her family. She loves the life she built. I can't imagine there is anything she would give it up for. Her green eyes roll, and she pushes a wayward curl out of her face with a huff.

"Why?" I asked, climbing out of Kano's lap. He lets me go, feeling secure with our deal. Then, I walk over to Aston, and she holds my hands.

"Because, like Roxie said, Earth sucks. It was always a grind, and I had to work so hard to prove myself to everyone. I was constantly attached to my phone and couldn't eat breakfast without posting about the eggs from the fancy grocery store or workout without going live to show everyone my poor form. All so I could support what I actually wanted to do, which was make art and teach art. It wasn't good enough for my dad. I had to do it all, and I had to do it all the Andrews way." She sighs, squeezing my hands reassuringly, "I love my family, Vera, but they weren't this big support group you thought they were. You were. You always believed in me, supported me. You were the reason I made it as far as I did and got out from under my father's thumb. You're practically my sister. I wouldn't want to leave you here alone."

The tears burn behind my eyes, and I let them fall. Something inside me must have shaken loose in that crystal field because a sob rips its way from my throat as I pull Aston into a hug. She holds me while I cry, and she cries a little bit, too, and when we pull apart, we wipe one another's tears.

"I love you, Ace," I say, my voice weak.

"I love you too, Vera. I'm happy to stay if we're in this together."

"Always," I promise, dragging her into a hug.

CHAPTER TWENTY-SIX

I won, but it was only the first battle in the war for my *ĝha*'s heart. She has agreed to stay in Wupeso with me, and my hearts beat in tandem with my excitement. The Baso Sheva continued to smile upon me when Vera's near-sister, Az-ton, admitted that she also wanted to stay here. I know this woman's importance to My Vera; I have seen it in how they treat one another. From the first night when Az-ton stood behind My Vera, even as she shook from fright, to this evening when Az-ton tried to hold me back from my own *ĝha* because my Vera needed space, I knew they had an unbreakable bond. This is much like the one I share with the sky warriors, Rihu and Royi. So it brings me great joy to have Az-ton stay.

Still, there is much work to be done with my Vera. She has started my second heart beating, and still, she does not understand what that means. She does not know I will do anything to make her happy and keep her safe. I would give her the world if I must, and if the only way she could have been happy was to return to Earth, I would have found a way. But I do not believe that is true. I think the Baso Sheva brought her here, to me, to give her another bond like the one she shares with Az-ton, but fuller, more complete. I believe the Baso Sheva knew she needed me. I could not send her away now anyway. I already love her.

"My Heart," I call to her, bringing myself closer to her side. "Will you accompany me to our home?"

Her skin pinches around her eyes, showing her tension, but she nods. She gives one final tangle to Az-ton before stepping toward me. Then, she walks away to hug Alba and Roxie and promises that she will be back tomorrow to help with the human stuff. After my *ĝha* said her goodbyes, we walked back home together.

My Vera was so exhausted she didn't murmur a word
before falling asleep in my arms. In her sleep, I see her true
face. Her lips are relaxed on quiet breaths. I brush a strand of
hair from her face, and knowing she will not hear it, I whisper,
"I love you already, My Vera."

CHAPTER TWENTY-SEVEN

Overnight, Blossom and Aston created a council of representatives to negotiate human interests on this new planet. This is why Blossom, Aston, Alba, Roxie, and Zach sit across the communal table from me, waiting for my "opening remarks." Aston's words.

I clear my throat and stall my time as long as possible. Then, finally, I say, "I know this situation isn't ideal, but with our likelihood of a return to Earth being so abysmally low, I think we should focus on integrating ourselves into the community here. I believe we can work together to improve this situation."

"Is that all?" Aston asks, staring me down like we're negotiating the price of a Craigslist couch.

"I believe so," I reply, with an equal amount of sass.

"Then, let me speak on behalf of the council." Aston starts, glancing at the others gathered. Each gives the nod or sound of approval, and then she begins, "The majority of the humans have agreed that staying in Wupeso is what will be best for our life, liberty, and happiness. However, we have stipulations we would like you to bring forth to Chief Kano."

"Who wants to return to Earth? What kind of stipulations?"

"Please, wait for the end of our opening remarks to ask your questions." Zach chimes in, sending Aston a conspiratorial wink.

Aston continues, "First, we want you to clarify with The Chief that the human population, and Blossom, reserve the right to refuse their *ĝhajo*, if one may appear."

I nod, thinking about Aston and Llazho and agreeing wholeheartedly that it should be her choice. Kano has treated me exceptionally well, but I don't know much about Aston's soulmate, and she should be given the option to get to know him and make her choice in her own time. She seems satisfied with my nod of assent because she continues.

"Next, we ask that The Chief provide help for the siblings who have found themselves stepping into guardian roles. According to the *peholoe*, there are trustworthy men and families here who would help with the children in a capacity similar to daycares or adoption if the guardian so chooses."

"That seems fair," I agree. Alba hums her agreement.

"Finally, the human faction of Wupeso would like the freedom to contribute to the tribe in the way they please or join the unmarried V`òllø women in travel expeditions as is traditional."

This was obviously the kicker. I didn't know about this tradition. And how would I? We had only been on this alien planet for a few days – days that we didn't even know the length of. We were stranded for good in a culture I knew so little about. Sure, I had learned about tangles and the different ways Kano tilts his head to agree or disagree. I learned about the sacred crystal fields, and I knew that they prayed to a higher deity. I even knew that they worked as a community for survival. But there was so much I didn't know or understand. Traditional V`òllø women were part of that.

"I thought the tribe didn't have any unmarried women other than the *peholoe*," I reply instead, realizing how insensitive I sound after the fact.

"There's one." Zach chimes in.

Blossom adds, "Soekho the Remaining. Only Zach has met her, but she was at our arrival."

"And she explores?" I ask.

"She used to," Zach answers again.

I drag my eyes back to Aston and search my best friend's face. I know her tells like the back of my hand, and I wonder if this is her desire. That she would like to travel and explore this world. But her left ear doesn't twitch when I stare her down, nor does she let out a stuttered exhale. I decide it must be future-forward thinking because we haven't even settled in here.

"I'll speak with Kano about it." I finally concede.

Aston smiles brightly, and I think it's the first time since we arrived that I saw that look on her face. It's one I'm familiar with – huge grin, nose wrinkle, sparkle alive and well in her eyes. "Then, that's all we have for you."

The council starts to break up when I say, "Wait, you never told me who doesn't want to stay."

"Daria," Alba says, doing the sign of the cross.

Daria is fully submerged in the steaming pool of blue-green water hidden within the fields of lavender-colored plants as tall as trees. Purple buds hold blue seeds and iridescent pollen that floats in the air, making me sneeze. By the time I had reached the pool, I was sniffling like mad and sneezing into my arm. My eyes water, and my face feels puffy. The steam helps, but only a little bit.

Daria's eyes are open, and she's staring ahead at the natural stone wall of the pool. The bubbles of her breath release slowly. Then, she shoots from the surface, splashing the edges of the land above. Her eyes lock directly onto me.

"What do you want?" She asks, taking a seat along the ledge on the pool walls. She pulls her knees into her chest protectively, and I know that she doesn't want to talk to me. I don't answer immediately, which seems to irk her. With a sigh, I pull the skirts of my alien dress up and stick my bare feet in the water. I lean back on my arms and sniffle back the river of sinus goo infecting me. I look at Daria, trying to read her even as she tries to block me out. Her magenta hair is soaked, but the kinky ringlets stand even against the weight of the water. She's not wearing any makeup, mostly because it doesn't seem to exist on this planet. And without it, she looks younger and less severe.

My voice is throaty when I finally speak, "I know you want to go home."

"I want to wake up." She replies, and I know exactly what she means. This feels like a dream, or a nightmare, depending on who you ask. One day, we're on the best up-and-coming space cruise, living lucky girl lives. The next, we're crash-landed on an alien planet with a dying race and no electricity. Which if you look on the bright side, still seems like we are living our lucky girl lives. Our little band of humans makes up the survivors of the attack on the *SS Herculean*. Our little band of humans ended up in the pod that found a safe landing planet. Our little band of humans found an alien race that wasn't hostile. The impossibilities are endless and profound. But then there's the dark side. You were on the nicest vessel in space. This shouldn't have happened at all. We all should have been on our way home by now, drinking mimosas by a pool or playing laser tag in a zero-gravity course. Families should be together or getting reunited soon. Everything should have gone according to plan.

"It's not a dream or a nightmare." I tell her, "It's our new reality."

"Blossom said there was a chance, but your decisions cut that in half."

The council didn't mention the new statistic, so this is the first time I'm hearing it is now around one percent. It's about the same percentage as being struck by lightning. Something that might not even apply in Wupeso.

"Is there someone you want to go home to?" I ask. Even though my family was garbage to me, I still loved them. The thought of never seeing them again made me sad. The way they will handle my estate, the conclusions they are sure to jump to, and the fact that I'm not there to change any of it makes me angry. Sure, I've resigned myself to stay, but that doesn't mean that my existence on Earth has ended. It doesn't mean I didn't lose people I care about. If anyone can understand what Daria is feeling, it's me. Or Aston. Or Alba. Or even Zach or Daria's sister.

When I look over at Daria, she has her head buried in her knees. Her magenta hair is like a halo around her. She peeks up at me, and her eyes shine with unshed tears. Then, she blinks, and it's gone. Her mouth tightens almost imperceptibly. Her voice is raw when she replies, "Probably not anymore."

"Do you want to talk about it?" It's an olive branch.

"No."

She doesn't say more, and I don't ask her to. Instead, I sit with Daria by the pool until she is ready to climb out. She gets dressed in alien garb, and I watch her pick at the material as it clings to her body. She hates it as much as every other difference in this place. Her disdain is clear on her face. She wants out of here, and she won't tell me why. Still, I was hoping to change her mind and convince her of the virtues of Wupeso, but now I'm not sure I have the power.

CHAPTER TWENTY-EIGHT

I wake in Kano's bed, alone. Then, I take the chance to look at his room through new eyes. His mattress is double the size of the one I have at home, and it sits on a flexible woven frame, propped up by crystals. The floors are wooden, but they always seem to stay warm, and I wonder how he does that. Or if all the floors in the alien's homes are heated this way. He doesn't keep any heavy blankets, and I figure that's because he sleeps like a raging fireplace. But he does have thin linen sheets. His bedroom is not particularly decorated. Aside from a device kind of like a windchime that hangs against the windows and a woven rug partially tucked under the bed, it's void of his things. Without him here, the whole space feels incomplete.

The sun is high in the sky now, painting lines of light across the floor. Kano's house is almost as far as we can get from the *Peholoe*'s hut, far enough that I can't even see the edges of the bay. But his view is perfect. The water outside his window crashes along the cliffside, looking smooth and glassy the further out you look. Gray-trunked trees with hot-pink leaves and pure white stems shade part of his fenced yard and act as a barrier to those evil lavender plants.

"Kano?" I call, wondering if he's hanging around. His name echoes around the space, but no response comes. So, I find my way out of the room.

His home is built so that there are no interior doors. Instead, the walls overlap in a way that keeps you from seeing the rest of the home. With his room like a circle, each subsequent room of his house is shaped like a crescent moon. Immediately outside his bedroom is a stone-lined bathing chamber. Water trickles in along the wall and cycles through a primitive drain in the floor. The next room is for storage. A spare outfit is folded neatly on a shelf, boots are stored under a bench, and multiple colorful outfits for a woman are stacked beside them. Spare sheets, tools, and a dozen crystal jars fill the rest of the shelves. I change out of my clothes and progress through the final door. In the main area of his home, there's a kitchen and living space, and the walls latch in multiple places like they can be opened to the outside air.

In the kitchen space, there is a wooden dish filled with fruit from my first day. The sparkly dust sits open in a dish beside it. I take a seat on the floor cushion and pull the fruit apart, sprinkling it with the salt-like substance. More windows fill this room, and the sun warms the space.

I'm so immersed in my meal that I don't even see Aston when she walks by or hear her when she slides through the cylindrical entry. She startles me when she sits on the cushion beside me, stealing a slice of my fruit.

With her mouth half-full, she says, "Rihu and Royi are taking us flying today. Let's go."

I swallow my own bite, "You hate heights."

Aston takes another slice of my fruit and chews voraciously. Her usually wild curls are tucked in a piece of unusual fabric and pinned to her head. Only a couple choice strands have been left out to coil around her face.

"The council decided. All the human adults are going, me included. All the kids are off with Zhalisee and Soehko today. So, the sky warriors are taking us all flying."

"Even Daria?" I ask, skepticism clear in my tone.

"It was her idea," Aston says, eating my final slice of fruit. I grumble about her eating my food before the surprise hits me about Daria's involvement in today's activity. Neither reaction matters as Aston drags me up from the floor and forces me outside. The walk-through town is slow, and I hate that I keep looking for a big, green man I haven't seen today. We're extra careful when we cross the chasm bridge. And then, I find myself standing at a bridge leading to a floating island I've never been to.

"There's no way." She says, watching the wooden planks swing in the breeze. We're hundreds of yards above the choppy waters below. The other human women have already crossed and stand on the other side about another hundred yards away. The wind is crazy up here, blowing without the trees or mountains to break their gusts. Aston is completely terrified.

"If I can go to space, you can cross a bridge." I encourage taking the first step onto the bridge. It rocks with my weight, and I watch Aston's face pale.

She hates heights. She always has. When I first moved to Vegas, I dragged her along for the zipline, and she refused to ride. When we took off into space, she squeezed her eyes closed tight and had a death grip on my hands. Every time she's on an airplane, she packs a bottle of pills, and climbing the steps to the karst makes her peaky. This time is no different. Even though everyone assures her it is safe, she has clear doubts.

"How safe can a wooden rope bridge really be?"

As if to prove the integrity, I took another three or four steps onto the bridge and hopped a couple times. She whimpers, and I hold out my hand to her.

"You can face massive alligator spiders, but not a measly little bridge? Come on! You're holding everyone up."

I'm right, and she knows I'm right, but she swears her legs feel like bags of jelly. She wants to step forward, but the fear freezes her in place. She looks back toward the loft and considers fleeing for her life. Then, her eyes catch sight of her *ĝha,* and she forces a foot forward. Aston takes one step toward me and grabs my hand. She tugs herself toward me with all her weight, and I tumble two steps further onto the bridge.

I can hear the women on the other side cheering like we've done some big feat. But it doesn't feel that way. Instead, their cheers let loose her panic, and I could practically see the blood pounding in her ears. Her eyes become unfocused. Her head wobbles. I pull her forward another step, and my hand is a death grip on Aston's. I pinch her forearm, and she hisses.

"You good?"

"Good," she says, letting me pull her across the bridge.

She keeps her eyes on me, counting her breaths to keep her mind occupied. Our feet shuffle along, and we make it to the other side by some miracle. Aston practically trips onto the solid land, and everyone claps at our arrival. I hold Aston up with a satisfied grin on my face, and she punches me on the side of my tit. But I'm nicer than her, so I don't retaliate. Instead, I stand up straight and try not to flinch back at the row of creepy birds. Now that's something I'm still not cool with.

Piercing gold eyes scan the horizon as their sharp talons scrape into the blueish dirt. You can sense the intelligence in their eyes as they click back and forth, communicating with one another. Their jet-black feathers ruffle as Rihu and Royi pet down the side of their necks. I can't imagine how they feel safe getting close to them. My one and only encounter with Lewe was more than enough. These birds are massive and terrifying, dwarfing the two warrior aliens who stand feet above us humans.

Rihu and Royi explain carefully about the black leather harnesses they've tucked around the sides of the birds, and I can barely listen. I don't want to do this. On the other hand,

Daria is happily listening mere feet from the sharp, curved beak of Rihu's mount. She quietly chirps under her voice, gaining the approval of the bird, like some kind of fairytale princess.

"Karo and Lari are both strong and impressive," Rihu says, his voice translated in my earbud. "We use the harnesses because their wings spread as far as five of me in height, and they are agile in the air. They can bank in as small a space as the palm of the healer Daria's hand."

Royi jumps in next, explaining how they are great for scouting, hunting, and battle. He points out all the vicious parts of their bodies and jokes about how lucky we are that they like us. I don't feel lucky. Especially when Lari caws aggressively in my direction.

When the safety speech is over, we are paired off into riding pairs and shown the course each of us will fly. All except me, who stands alone. The women buzz with excitement, and I'm standing on the edge, nibbling on my nail. Somehow, this attracts Rihu and Royi.

"Vera! Since you are alone, we will take you up first." Royi explains. I know little of these two alien men, and my skin crawls at the concept of climbing onto one of their beasts.

Rihu, whose color is only slightly different than his closest friend, elbows me gently, "Sorry Kano and Lewe couldn't make it. He had other responsibilities to attend to."

One of his eyes completely darkens in color, and I have to wonder if Rihu winked at me. A nervous laugh bubbles out of me, and I shake it off. He and his lookalike gently escort me toward their beasts, and the panic that started this morning revs up in my veins. I don't want to do this, but my feet keep moving.

Way too late, I respond, "It's okay. I'm sure Kano has a reason to be busy."

Royi nods, grabbing me by the hips and latching me onto his mount. The beast doesn't immediately attack, and I calm down a little. Rihu smiles in my direction, but unlike Kano, it doesn't make my heart flip in my chest. Royi jumps onto the beast behind me and latches himself in while Rihu mounts his own animal. My heart beats like hummingbird wings in my chest and only quickens as the birds shuffle along to the island's edge.

The wind is loud against the edge of the island, and Rihu shouts into my ear, "Are you ready?"

I shake my head from side to side, but it's too late. The bird falls off the edge, opening its wings to glide. I pinch my eyes shut, and my heart drops to my belly. My hands are wrapped so tightly around the harness I can feel them cramping. This big bird is going to drop me. He will return me to the chasm where Lewe never should have saved me. But then, the ride smooths out. When I open my eyes again, Lari glides along the water. The animal tilts the edge of a wing into the water before soaring up into the sky. When I look back at Royi, he's grinning from ear to ear. The energy field surrounding him crinkles against the wind, and his hair flows freely behind him.

My same nervous laugh turns into a cackle, and I let my arms out wide. My abs shake as I hold myself up against the wind, but my limbs feel weightless. All the panic flees my body as the bird whips and dives. Inside the harness, it feels like a roller coaster. The drop is terrifying, but ultimately, I'm safe. Lari makes a few extra turns, giving me a bird's eye view of the island. It's beautiful. Lari is beautiful.

The crystal fields look magical, mirrored only by the lavender plants on the opposite side of the island. Our silver escape pod in the bay looks like a toy, out of place in such a natural landscape. And the chasm seems as dark and terrifying as it is. The houses disappear above the floating islands, but the landscape looks the same, strange and beautiful.

Lari uses her iridescent wings to create circles smaller and smaller before landing on the ledge of the island and stepping further into the island with a ruffle of her wings. Rihu dismounts, but Royi helps me down. Offering me a steady arm. We walk back toward the group together, but they both stop me in the dark of the trees. The birds weren't nearly as scary as this moment.

"You couldn't have a better *ĝha* than Kano," Royi tells me, his eyes searching my own. Rihu pulls me to face him.

"And if you choose him, our people will choose you the same," Rihu explains.

I can't explain why tears prick at my eyes, but I blink them back. Then, with both hands, I grab one of their horns and drag them down into some semblance of a tangled hug. I didn't realize how worried I had been about the V`òllø's acceptance. The sky warriors' promise was precisely what I needed to hear.

Aston finds me cuddling the warriors' horns in the trees, and she snorts in my direction. I break away from them as the heat rises to my cheeks. Catching up with Aston, she wraps an arm around my waist.

"When did you become such a softie?" She asks, dragging me back to the humans.

Brushing away a wayward tear, I say, "I don't know."

CHAPTER TWENTY-NINE

My people have many traditions that I appreciate. We are community-minded people with faith built into our bodies. The world gives us life, and we promise to give it back. As often as we can, my people pray to the Baso Sheva. We dedicate slivers of the sun's light to our faith and community. We work together against the struggles we face. From traditional rising prayer amongst the crystals to the bonding ceremonies of *ĝhajo*, we are a people of tradition.

This is why, though my pride begs me not to, I go to the neighboring village to extend the invitation to my *r̈ ůsad'ù*. I felt anger because the neighboring chief denied my requests time and time again, knowing he would be dooming my village. Still, the Baso Sheva insists I invite them. Tradition states that all known V`òllø must be asked to witness the bonding ceremony, or it will not be blessed. I set aside my pride for My Vera, my soul, my second heart.

Or, at least, I will. If Kethi Rogeshu decides to answer my visit. Valkarra is smaller than my own island, though it is home to more people. They are not as traditional. Their homes are all made of mud and clay from the mountains that trap them on both sides, and they have no floating islands protecting them from the sun. The mountains that trap them also provide for them, though. Freshwater, clay, and game are abundant in their land. It's why we maintain peace with them.

I'm waiting by their temple, a building they built for their worship of the Baso Sheva. I refuse to enter the space because I don't think Baso Sheva intended us to worship her in the dark. She gave us her fields for a reason. They strengthen us in the light. The longer I wait, the antsier I become to return to My Vera. I left her earlier to make this trip and would curse Kethi a *lushi* if he kept me from seeing her eyes fall closed tonight.

140

I am about to give up on tradition when he finally shows. Kethi is shaped much like me, tall, even for a V`òllø, and wide, but that is where our similarities end. While I am the color of *rishi* leaves, he is the color of the soil. A blueish-gray sheen covers his skin, pulled through with tattoos of silver and eyes like ice crystals. His hair is long, and silver and short patches cover his sharp jawline. His horns curve back over his head in the same silver as his tattoos.

He taps his horn to mine in greeting, and I grunt at his casualness. He keeps me from my *ĝha* for his silly games.

"I still cannot send my women Kano Rogeshu." He says, walking along a well-worn path to their crystal fields. I keep step with him while I try to explain.

"I have no need of your women," I say, knowing my voice betrays my annoyance. Keeping my horns high, I continue, "I am here to invite you and your people to my *R̈ uṣad'ù.*"

Kethi stops in the path without warning, and my frustration grows. He is younger than me by many seasons and does not hold the same respect close to his hearts. The blue of his eyes narrows toward me.

"You actually found women?" He is surprised and intrigued. Giddy excitement begins to flow out of him, and I step back.

"The Baso Sheva provided women. Though they are small and different. My Vera is actually the tallest of them," I brag, pointing at the spot on my chest where my *ĝha* reaches.

"Vera," Kethi murmurs, pulling a growl from my throat. I have always been a level-headed man. But her name on his lips makes me wish to tear them off. Kethi puts forth his horns apologetically. "Tell me about them."

We spend hours talking about human women. I explained how small they were and that they seemed weak, but My Vera could withstand poison and catch herself from falling into the chasm. I tell him about Blossom, the sun-thetic woman with her skin of pink metal who helps us communicate. I tell him about the giant silver pod that brought them here and the names of all the women I remember. By the end, Kethi promises to attend my *R¨uṣad'ù*, if only to meet these human women. We pray together among the crystals before I depart. The Baso Sheva is pleased.

CHAPTER THIRTY

Kano still isn't home when the sky darkens. Aston walked home with me, what I suspect was over an hour ago since the sky was still bright then. I had already eaten dinner with the humans and played a round of poker in which I won full custody of my lucky cards. Then, we played another few games before Aston declared she needed a walk. We talked like we were back on Earth all the way home.

Aston told me about her situationship with Llazho – bad. Then, I told her about mine with Kano – good? Then, we talked about Zhalisee and the *peholoe*. She told me about Pa coming to the loft every morning before the sun to care for the baby so Alba could sleep. She told me about Daria's younger sister, the first human to be allowed to touch a training weapon. She tells me about the other women with mates and how quickly Cerridwen fell for Zhu. And I told her about what happened in the crystal fields and how much Kano finding the cards meant to me.

Aston admitted she saw them fall out of my pocket when I went after Alba on the ship, and she left the pod to get them for me. She said I would need all the luck I could get.

I run through the entire conversation again while waiting for Kano to get home. I had never been a really anxious person before. When I used to dance, confidence was key. Then, in poker, all my emotions were weapons that could be used against me. So, I learned to keep all those emotions on the inside. Yet, I find myself pacing the wall of windows in Kano's bedroom, watching the horizon for a sign of him or his scary bird.

I haven't seen him at all today, and it sets my brain catastrophizing. Maybe he fell into the chasm. Perhaps some evil monster, I don't know about, got to him. Maybe he realized I'm not actually his *ĝha,* and he doesn't want to be with me anymore, so he ran away. I know so little about this planet that I quickly spiral into madness. What if he's been captured by other aliens? Mean ones like the monsters on the *SS Herculean.* What if he's hurt? What if he's dead?

I'm moments from walking out the door. I've strapped my shoes back on, and I'm trying to find one of those shards of glowing crystal he keeps tucked in the bedside table when I hear him step into the bedroom. My face snaps to his, and I watch the emotions flicker over his face like movie panels. Exhaustion pulls at his frame, dragging him downward, in on himself. His horns droop forward, and his tail drags along the floor. Then, he sees me standing there, still awake, and surprise flickers in his eyes. The color widens and narrows in on me as if he can't quite believe I'm still awake. Then, his smile spreads slowly across his face. His shoulders roll back, and his delight that I'm awake and in his room is a palpable force between us.

I straighten, dropping the crystal back in the drawer, before shoving it closed. His grin only grows. I step back against the table, and he eats up the room in two steps. Then, he's sweeping me off my feet and into his arms. He crushes me to his chest, and my legs naturally wrap around his waist. I wrap my arms around him like a spider monkey, and all my anxiety washes away in his arms.

He brushes back my hair, pressing his lips to my hairline. He's whispering soft nothings in my ear, and I wish for my earbud, but it's all the way across the room, so I only understand a few words. He calls me his *ĝha,* his *sodza* – soul, his Vera. He says something about our wedding, but I don't understand it. Then, he presses another kiss to my hairline and slides me down his body.

"I missed you," I admit, unsure of the location of his own earbud. It must be in his ear because he beams. He's always so pleased when I share how I feel with him, and I can't help but think that makes him nothing like human men. My last boyfriend hated when I worried about him. He would get upset with me when he'd get home late, and I waited up. He would yell and say I should be asleep. If I told him I missed him, he would answer with something akin to, "Of course you did." Rather than the much-needed –

"I missed you too," Kano replies, tucking my earbud in my ear. I didn't even realize he had the opportunity to retrieve it. I had been so occupied with the past. He tucks a strand of my hair behind my ear before carrying me to the bed. "It was a long day without you in it."

My heart calms in my chest at his words. Kano is nothing like my last boyfriend. In fact, I think the idea of cheating on me the way that guy did would be abhorrent to my big green man. So, exercising a modicum of trust, I ask, "Where did you go?"

"I had to visit Valkarra. It is tradition to invite all known V`òllø people to a *R ̈uṣad'ù*. Their attendance bears witness to our bond."

His thumbs rub soothing circles on my sides, but they still when I stiffen at his words. The last few days had been so full of adjustments I had forgotten about Kano's announcement at our welcome dinner. He intended to marry me in only a few more days. *Was I ready for that?*

"And? Are they coming?" I ask, slipping out of his arms. This clearly confuses him, but I wrap my arms around my knees and close off my face. Since I visited the crystal fields, I have shown my feelings more plainly. I wouldn't continue to do that tonight.

"Yes, Kethi Rogeshu has agreed to attend with a small group of his people."

My exterior stiffens, but his doesn't. If anything, he does the opposite. His hands reach for my leg, wrapping around my ankle. He tugs my feet forcefully into his lap, rubbing the arches and forcing a small groan from my lips. On Earth, I was used to being on my feet, but this little island was long and rocky. It was a daily hike to climb the steps of the karst to reach the *peholoe* loft, and I tended to reach my step count long before noon. My ankles had been swollen since the second day, but I figured I would get used to it over time. Because of all this, his warm hands felt like heaven. Kano worked his way from my feet, up my calves, then to the front of my thighs. When he pulled me into his arms and rubbed my shoulders, my body had utterly thawed against him.

"What did you do this light cycle?" He asks, his voice husky in my ear. I gave him the meadow report, telling him of Aston's bravery and the exhilaration of flight. I told him about the sea breeze and the walk home. I was poetic in my descriptions of his island and the view I'd been given. His hands worked my muscles the whole time, massaging out the knots I'd held onto.

He finishes his slow massage and tugs me to his chest. He rests his chin on the top of my head and leans us back against the headboard. I can feel his hardness against me, but he doesn't put any pressure on me. Instead, he seems content to hold onto me, and I'm satisfied to rest in his arms.

"So, the *R̈uṣad'ù* is happening then?" I ask when I'm finished telling him about the day. I twist my head to look up at him, and I can see the tiredness in his eyes.

Still, he says, "Yes, My Vera."

I dream of poofy white wedding gowns and strange jade eyes that night.

CHAPTER THIRTY-ONE

I wake to the grating sound of Az-ton's squeal. I roll to the side to pull my *ĝha* to my chest, but I find her side of the bed cold. The first beams of sunlight pierce my eyes, and I can feel my color move to block it out. I realize that My Vera has been awake for a while, and I wonder how long Az-ton has been here. Az-ton's voice carries like the hiss of the *d'iru*, filling the walls of my home with its high-pitched buzz as she tells my *ĝha* of her excitement.

My *ĝha*'s voice soothes my nerves, "Az-ton, quiet. Kano is still sleeping."

"Uhm, I'm sorry! I'll try not to be excited about my chance to plan a human-alien wedding."

"No one asked you to plan it," My *ĝha* huffs. Even from the other room, I can see how her arms are likely crossed over her chest. Her brows are probably narrowed in her friend's direction. I think of how I will be bonded to her soon, and then I wonder if that means I will wake to Az-ton's many noises often.

"You didn't have to," Az-ton says, still much too loud for me to sleep through, "You're my best friend, and events happen to be what I'm best at."

I decide I've heard enough from my room and dress quickly before joining them at my table. Entering the room, they stop speaking entirely. It is odd for them both to be so quiet. I freeze in the doorframe, feeling unwelcome, before dropping a kiss on the top of My Vera's head and grabbing some fruit. Az-ton's eyes, a color similar to mine, glare in my direction. That is when I realize I truly am unwelcome. *In my own home, nonetheless.*

"I will get some breakfast and be on my way," I say, picking up some *vau* fruit. "I'm sure Kethi Rogeshu will be here shortly."

"Kethi?" Az-ton asks, looking between us.

My Vera explains for the both of us as I slide out the door, "Another village's leader."

I was right, of course. I step outside my home, and as if by starcraft, Kethi appears. When we spoke the day before, it was only the two of us, but today he is accompanied by two other V`òllø. Liro Sheho and Nohktir Sheho, his chosen advisors. They all tilt their horns at me before falling into step beside me. They all know where I am headed since it is common knowledge that our crystal fields are my refuge.

"Must be nice, waking with your *ĝha*. I don't think I've heard of a day where the great Kano Rogeshu didn't wake before the sun." Liro teases. I do not drop to his level, keeping my eyes on the trail ahead.

"You made quick travel," I say instead, though I wished it had taken them longer to arrive. It's not that we didn't like the Valkarran people. It's that the Valkarran interpreted Baso Sheva's gifts differently and acted differently because of it.

I note the wonder on their faces as we walk through town. Evidence of the festival I called for is all around us. Every home is decorated with flowers and gems in celebration of the upcoming *R¨uṣad'ù*. Over the past light cycles, a market of everyone's favorite creations has been created along the bay's beaches. Then, there was the music. Crystalline chimes hang on the porches of homes, catching the wind and creating a background sound for the instruments played by my people. Those who are not making preparations or tending to stalls, dance, sing, or play *b'oshiphi* or *reru*. I see the young V`òllø boys with the older human children preparing a battle of entertainment for our reception, and they wave at us as we pass.

"The skies were clear. A blessing of the Baso Sheva." Kethi says, though his eyes scan my village. I can only imagine he and his advisors seek *ĝhajo* of our new women. Why else would they attend my *R̈ůṣad'ù* after denying me the opportunity to meet with their few eligible women? Bitterness fills me, only to be extinguished by my blessings as we arrive at the crystal fields.

Kethi dismisses his advisors, and we walk into the fields together. Unlike Valkarra, we did not erect a V`òllø-made temple. Instead, the shallow cave where the ice and fire crystals meet acts as our place of worship. It blocks the worst of the elements and maintains a pleasant temperature. I kneel in the shards and bow my head in prayer. Or at least, I try to, but a particular visitor divides my attention.

"Will you host your *R̈ůṣad'ù* here?" He asks, perusing the shallow cave.

I imagine it decorated in flowers and light, the crystals reverberating with the bonding music. I imagine My Vera dressed in traditional *R̈ůṣad'ù* clothes, kneeling across from me in the shadow of the crystal cave. I imagine the smell of fresh *rulo* flowers, crushed under the feet of our witnesses. I even imagine Pa and Hoga standing before us and walking us through the vows to our Baso Sheva.

"Yes. The fields of Baso Sheva are the most beautiful of places to host a *R̈ůṣad'ù*."

Kethi seems to imagine what I see before nodding in agreement. I returned to my prayers, thanking the Baso Sheva for my *ĝha*'s understanding the evening before. Then, Kethi interrupts again.

"Sheva above, how do you kneel in this grit?" He grumbles, standing from the ground. Beside him, there is a mat he could use instead, but he does not. No. Kethi paces the sacred space, allowing the shards to crunch loudly under his boots, letting huffed breaths fall from his lips. I return to praying, ignoring his constant noise.

"How uncouth must you be to pray this long to the Baso Sheva? Has she not blessed you with *ĝhajo* for your men? Hasten your prayers." He grumbles, walking toward the shallow cave. His blue hands run over the walls with curiosity, and I try my best to focus even as he disturbs the sacred place. His eyes travel from the art carved into the walls to find me kneeling.

"Unbelievable. We will head into a third sliver of the sun soon enough. Can you please finish your prayers? I would like to meet the humans."

I smirk. Giving one final thanks to the Baso Sheva, I stand from the sand and dust it from my knees.

"Let us go and make the formal introductions."

"Oh, God. There's more of them?" The human Roxie exclaims as I walk through the entry to the *peholoe* loft with Kethi and his advisors in tow. Since the women arrived, I have been getting to know their names and small facts about them, like I know all my people. Roxie is a brave and outspoken human who brings energy to the group. The women turn to see me and the new arrivals from Valkarra. My mate smiles in my direction, but she holds a swath of fabric and a needle in her lap. So, she does not rise to meet me.

"Let me introduce Kethi Rogeshu and his advisors, Liro and Nohktir. They are from our neighboring village, Valkarra. They will be here until the *R̈uṣad'ù* is concluded."

"Kethi?" Roxie says, looking at him as I do. Annoyance is written clearly on her human features.

"Yes, *sà*. And you are?" Kethi replies, his eyes filled with delight. His lips tilt up in a smirk, and I watch Roxie's head tilt. My Vera seems to glance between them with a knowledgeable look.

"Commander Roxie Holt." Her hand brushes the handle of her weapon, and my eyes dart to My Vera in question. She only shakes her head in my direction. The human Roxie's hands steady and move from her weapon as she walks across the room, inspecting Kethi like a dead fish along the beach.

We all watch with curiosity as she runs a hand up his abdomen and chest. I see the flash of light under his shirt and hear his second heart begin to beat; the color of his eyes grows slightly. His pupils flash wide and then narrow to almost indistinguishable points on the woman touching his chest. Roxie simply raises onto her tip-toes and peels back Kethi's upper lip. She tilts her head at his fangs before pursing her lips and dropping back to the floor.

"Something is different about you. In time, I will figure it out," Roxie says before rejoining the other women. Kethi only stares forward at his *ĝha* in disbelief as she saunters back to the group. Immediately, the women begin chattering again, speaking of the human twist they plan to put on our *R̈uṣad'ù*.

I don't know what he sees from his *ĝha*, but for once, Kethi is stunned into complete silence, and I can't help but thank the Baso Sheva for the miracle.

CHAPTER THIRTY-TWO

Hoga beats me in another game of Neked'I. As usual, I thought I had her. My circle was built entirely, and I was ready to uncover the Kano chips, but she stole a fragment from my ring to complete her own. Therefore, activating the Baso Sheva chip and winning the game once again. The only difference between this game and the first was that she could tell me what I did wrong. But she didn't.

"You get better and better each game," Hoga told me instead, shuffling the chips.

I wasn't convinced. As far as I could tell, this game was built for only Hoga to win. After our flying day, I played two games with her and some of the other *peholoe,* and it didn't make a difference. Hoga won every time, never explaining her strategy. Rra, another one of the *peholoe* women, had leaned over and whispered that she was sure Hoga cheated. Pa said Hoga earned her luck the hard way, and winning *roshev* was proof from the Baso Sheva that she still held it. But after losing so many games, my frustration mounted.

"What if we played poker?" I asked, pulling my lucky cards from a pocket in my trousers. After staying at Kano's the first night, I had given in to V`òllø fashion. The linen clothes were lighter and more relaxed. They covered more of my skin and protected me from that excess radiation Blossom had told us about. Since we didn't have sunscreen, all humans agreed that good skin coverage was necessary. The clothier Zhalisee introduced me to made good on her promise to provide me some clothes via a package this morning, and that's how I found myself the proud owner of a pair of wide-leg, pocketed, homemade trousers, the same color as the ice crystals in the fields.

"Beh!" Hoga says, tilting her horns back in a way I've learned is dismissive. "Your human game is too simple."

"You're scared you will lose at my game the same way I lose at yours," I mutter, tucking my cards back in my pocket. Another thing I've learned over the past few days is that fighting with Hoga is a waste of time. Like with Neked'I, she always wins.

Hoga sighs, "If you really wish to win, why don't you play in town? Tonight, the festival will have many games. Maybe you can welcome the Valkarran visitors with your human *poker*."

I glance at the table where the women are getting ready to join the festival tonight. It has been going on since Kano announced it, with each day themed on old V`òllø traditions. It was why the entire town was singing or dancing in the streets. Tonight, the festival is all about camaraderie, loyalty, and friendship. It is why Kano had to leave yesterday to invite the people of Valkarra. If they weren't invited to this part of the celebration, it would be some kind of political slight.

Still, I didn't want to go. Part of me knew if I planned to be the alien queen – still getting used to that – then I'd have to show up for the people. But the part of me who still wasn't happy with the less than one percent chance of escape wanted to hide out with Hoga and get stomped in Neked'I all night. My eyes met Aston's across the room, and she patted the spot on the floor next to her. Grumbling, I stood from my game and found my way to the table.

The table is covered in odd-colored concoctions built from food, water, and plants. Humans are adaptable, and our females are full of ingenuity. So, dump us on a strange planet where the men and elders care for us, and what will we do? Create makeup from scratch, learn to sew our clothes, cook new foods, and share our personal catalogs of information while doing it.

"Does anyone else get a vibe from the Valkarran guys?" Roxie asks for the fifth time today, slicking back her hair with the gel from inside a cactus-like plant. Everyone mumbles some version of no, except me, who had noticed the unique look on Kethi's face under Roxie's hand. With my validation, she says, "Right? Total weirdos."

Clara, the milky-eyed woman, jokes, "I don't know. That Kethi guy sounds hot."

I can practically see Roxie tense and wonder if she feels some weird pull. Since I started sleeping in Kano's bed, I've noticed a bond growing between us. It's gone from me avoiding him like the plague, to worrying about being too in his space, to missing him when we're not attached at the hip. Like now, I'm surrounded by human women, who help me feel like a human again, but something feels off because he's not here. It's like a line of tension under my skin pulled taut whenever we're apart. And for the second day in a row, we've been apart all day.

I've been with the human women, planning our wedding – or *R̈ ůṣad'ù*, or whatever – helping with the kids and getting everyone settled in. Kano's been with the visitors, hosting a tour, introducing them to the people, and integrating them into the festival. We're both doing what we need to be doing, but I want to say forget it and jump into bed with him.

"Ope, she's dreaming about Kano again," Aston says, swiping a hand in front of my face. My lips turn down at my transparency. Have I really become that easy to decode?

"How are you and Llazho?" I ask, turning the tables on Aston, slightly hoping to hear this itchiness beneath my skin is normal.

Aston groans, applying some dark blue mixture to her eyelashes, "Aliens can be assholes too, it seems."

I frown at this before realizing I'm still transparent and schooling my face into its usual mask.

"It's like he tells me what to do, you know?" Aston asks, checking her application in the bowl of water. "He never asks me how I am or if I'm adjusting well to this weird alien world. He doesn't ask about my hobbies or what I like to do on Earth. He barely even calls me by my name. He's like, "*Ĝha* this and *Ĝha* that. *Ĝha*, come fishing with me. *Ĝha*, don't go near Rihu or Royi. *Ĝha*, stop going to Kano's hut *with the first sliver of the sun*. It's frustrating."

Cerridwen is the one to respond, giving a sympathetic hum. "Sorry, Aston. I wish I knew Llazho's problem to help you, but Zhu is kind. I want to be next to him every time we are apart because he makes this new life simpler. It's so easy."

Aston smacks her hand down on the table, "See! That. That's what I want. Why can't Llazho make it easy for me? Why does he have to be so demanding?"

I struggle to find an answer for my best friend because Kano isn't demanding either. If anything, he's set on keeping me happy with him. He's committed to me like no man has ever been. To the point where he committed to marry me within three days of meeting me. Two of which we barely spoke.

I finally settled on, "I'm sorry, Aston."

The other ladies at the table murmur their agreement, but my friend shakes her head. She brushes her hair back with a sigh, "Don't be. That's Llazho's job."

I finally won my first game of Neked'I at the festival. It may not have been against Hoga, but it was against Kano and Kethi. The two big, bad leaders. Zhalisee cheers as I pull the Kano chips together with the Baso Sheva, protected and active in my circle. The leaders realized they had lost, and the people cheered and laughed at my victory. Kethi groans, letting himself fall back into the grass behind him, but Kano smiles across the table at me.

It's a beautiful night in the center of Wupeso. Music and singing can be heard from every corner of the village. Colorful lights line the streets, and children run and play along the hillsides. The warm breeze swims through the tall blue grass we're sitting in. I run my fingers over the baby blue roots, feeling the smooth, waxy texture under my fingers. Then, Kano catches my hand, squeezing it in his own.

My heart races at his touch. When I look at him, his eyes are already on me, ready to catch my gaze. The world seems to fall away as we stare into one another's eyes. The pleasant thrum of excitement from my win fades, replaced with hope for this new bond with Kano. His smile grows softer, and he leans toward me, capturing my lips with his own.

Sparks cascade down my skin, creating that familiar flutter inside my chest. His free hand comes to my face, tilting me up to deepen our kiss, and I feel like I'm floating in space. He nips my bottom lip, and I part my mouth for him, anticipating the feel of his tongue against mine. But it never comes.

Kano's face rips away from mine. Confusion is tight in his eyes as we both realize what happened. The twins stand there with Demi and two V`òllø boys, staring at the frisbee-like disc beside Kano. They are all frozen in fear as they realize they accidentally hit Kano with the toy. Then, Kethi bursts out laughing, picking up the not-frisbee and tossing it over the next hill.

Kano looks at me with disbelief, and my own laughter spills from my lips, drawing his smile back out. I've found he can never be upset if I smile. There's a sense of unity and joy in the air, and I feel drunk on its effects. The situation feels normal for the first time since arrival on this planet. The way the human children play with the V`òllø, as if it's always been done, the way the V`òllø men politely offer and gift objects they've made to the human women – it feels right.

"What are you thinking about, My Vera?" Once again, Kano takes my hand in his, pulling me from the ground. Then, with his free hand, he brushes the flakes of grass from my rear, and my heart melts.

On Earth, I couldn't be a tender person. I'd been thrown into the cold too often to let my guard down or trust someone. But since being here, Kano found way after way to make me melt. In every case, he knew exactly what to do. Reaching up on my tippy-toes, I answer him with a kiss.

I try to tell him 'thank you' with my lips pressed to his to make him understand how much he's done for me. To make him comprehend the sense of rightness I feel tonight.

I didn't want to attend the festival, but he knew that. It's why he picked me up at the loft, even though it meant he had to walk all the way back across town. It's why he packed a jacket Zhalisee made for me that he would never need or use. It's why he brought me straight to the Neked'I table where I could feel at home, and it's why he challenged me to a game so I'd be forced to beat him.

Kano knew how to make this night perfect, and I wanted to communicate that with more than a kiss.

"Do you think we can sneak home for the night?"

My eyes must communicate my need because Kano sweeps me into his arms and carries me *home.*

CHAPTER THIRTY-THREE

We barely made it back. My Vera started kissing my neck when the sounds of the festival began to fade, moving her way up to a sensitive part behind my ear. When we were safely away from the chasm, her legs went around my waist, and our lips locked. This kiss was like pouring fire into my veins. The want and desire I had been carefully suppressing filled me. My cock thickened in my trousers, pressing against her core.

At the front door of my home, I press her against the door, grinding my hardness against her cunt. A small gasp breaks her lips at the feel of my desire, and I see her face in the moonlight. Her eyes are half-mast, shining bright with lust. Her lips are parted, revealing that pink tongue I want to taste again. With one arm banded around her middle, I force the door open with the other. Carrying her inside, I capture her lips as we go.

The door is kicked shut, and the sounds of the festival filling the streets of Wupeso die, leaving us panting in the dim light of a glowing crystal. She nips at my bottom lip, and I open to her, feeling the brush of her tongue against my own, tasting the sweet *tsare* on her lips. Kneeling on the floor, I sweep the fruit from the table in one arc, setting my *ĝha* upon it. Her hands unwind from my neck, trailing down my body to brush my cock through my trousers. She works the strings, and I groan against her neck.

"Touch me again," I demand, placing hot kisses on the delicate skin of her neck. Her hand brushes across my cock again, and a shiver works its way down my spine.

"My Vera," I breathe, reaching for the tunic button at the nape of her neck. Her soft hair glides over my hand, and it feels like inner peace. My fingers thread through it, tilting her eyes up to meet my own, and I wonder if she sees how I feel for her. I wonder if she can see my love and need for her. Now, I want her to see how I love that she is a leader for the humans. I want her to notice my affection for the way she plays games. I want her to feel my love for her stubbornness or my lust when her body is against mine. My hand tightens in her hair, and her eyes widen. Then, her hands tug me down for another kiss.

Between each press of our lips, she whispers, "Touch. Me."

I obey without question, sliding my hands under her tunic and dragging the fabric over her sides. Breaking the kiss long enough to remove her tunic, my lips find hers again before cutting a trail down her body. Miniscule bumps appear on her skin, pebbling and disappearing as I press her body against the table. My thumbs rest under her breasts, brushing over her nipples gently. She moans, her hips rotating beneath me.

"Kano, please," She begs, making my cock harden further. My Vera does not usually let her feelings known to me so quickly.

My lips close around her nipple, drawing it into my mouth, laving it with my tongue. Her hips shot off the table once again, and a desperate moan tumbles from her lips. Releasing her first nipple, I kiss my way across her chest, giving the other some much-needed attention. Then, with careful pressure, I bite, watching her face. This moan is the sound I want to hear for the rest of my life. It's musical and lilting and carries through my home, blessing the walls with its vibrations.

I nip and suck and bite her nipple, drawing a hand down her soft stomach and removing her pants. I draw a line down her body and her muscles flex and curve beneath my palm. My Vera is so soft and smooth. It's intoxicating.

Her hips reach for me, seeking friction, and I'm happy to oblige. I stroke across the seam of her pussy, feeling her wetness coat my fingers. A low rumble starts in my chest as the scent fills the air. My Vera is all things right and blessed. Her smell, like spice and musk, drags me in. I need more.

My palms come to her inner thighs, spreading her wide beneath me. My Vera is perfect in all things. A witty mind, a leader's heart, a perfect pussy. Pink and glistening, spread open, wet, and ready for me. She leans up on her elbows, and I wonder if she'll tell me to stop. But she doesn't. My hands shift to her hips, pulling her to the end of the table, and she moans.

My hot breath is on her pussy when I ask, "Is this okay?"

She nods emphatically, biting back a whimper. I watch carefully as her pussy drips for me. Then, I taste. The flavor of Vera explodes on my tongue, pulling a groan from my throat that pleasantly rumbles against her skin. My tongue glides from her entrance up to the bundle of nerves she circled that night in the bathhouse. Her hands shoot to my horns, gripping them tightly and pressing my face against her. I use my thumbs to spread her pussy, centering my attention on this little bead of pleasure. A tentative suck rewards me with my favorite of her moans. A wave of wetness drips from her center, and my tongue dips to taste it.

I am harder than the cliffs, but I want to feel My Vera, my soul, come apart beneath me. My mouth returns to her clit, and her moans grow louder, emboldening me. As I suck and lick her clit, I slip a finger inside her entrance, feeling the texture of her inner walls grip me. My Vera has become an open book under my ministrations, directing me with her moans of pleasure on how she likes to be touched. I add a second finger, curling them against a spongey patch inside her.

Her thighs flex around me, pinning me to her body. Her gasping moan turns into, "I'm coming. I-I'm coming."

160

Pure satisfaction rushes through me as I help her through the waves of her orgasm. Her taste is perfect, bathing my tongue and pushing me forward. But it's not enough. I want more. Her legs shake around me, and I won't stop, causing her to come on my tongue again. She's panting, pulling my horns, grinding on my face as my fingers thrust into her hot cunt, dragging her to the edge repeatedly until I finally pull her over, and she screams my name in her climax.

It's a prayer and a plea when she sighs, "Kano. Kano, yes." It is music to my ears. After she climaxes on my tongue for the third time, I slowly take my fingers out of her, cleaning her gently with my tongue, savoring the tiny shudders that work through her body as she tries to catch her breath.

I sit back on my feet, looking over my *ĝha*'s pleasure-addled body with admiration. My Vera's skin is still flushed and glowing, her pussy swollen and pink. Her chest rises and falls, jiggling her breasts in the cool air. Her long strands of silken hair are a halo around her head. My stiffness becomes painful, and I press a hand to it with a groan, ignoring my own pleasure to bask in hers.

CHAPTER THIRTY-FOUR

Three times. He made me come three times with his *tongue*. I giggle in disbelief before pulling in a shaky breath. My boyfriends on Earth could never. I let my hands fall to my sides, feeling the cool table beneath me as another aftershock skitters through my body. Pulling my head from the table is a feat in itself, but I do, finding Kano's eyes locked on my body.

My pussy clenches on air at the sight. Kano's muscled chest and abdomen are on display, glowing slightly with two matching silvery tattoos. One hand presses into his thigh, while the other is against his cock, which is still painfully restrained by his trousers. I feel like I got dunked in that Helleboralis stuff because my blood boils. I've come three times and still want to do filthy things with him.

My legs feel like gelatin as I try to stand, and I decide against it, straddling his wide lap instead. I move his hand away and drip at the sound of his groan. Making quick work of his strings, I wrap my hand around his bare cock. It's like an electrical pulse shoots through me, straight to my clit at the contact. I moan.

His eyes flick to mine, and there is so much color I can't even find his pupil. The intensity of his lust shines through. My body matches it. I tighten my grip on his cock, feeling it swell in my hand. Kano grunts, breathing through his nose as the muscles of his stomach tighten. A bead of precum glistens on the head. I gently move down his body, intending to reciprocate, but Kano jumps, pulling me further into his lap.

His cock brushes my pussy, and I moan against the tattoo on his chest. It seems familiar, but the post-O haze messes with my mind. I trace it with my finger, grinding gently against his hardness. It seems to glow under my touch, and that's when it hits me. They're like the runes on the Neked'I chips. I sit back. Two squares are interlocked on their points, with a single line drawn down the center and a tiny circle at the shape's bottom. Each figure is the size of my hand.

"The Kano runes," I whisper. The lines are perfect, completely absent of human error, and the ink is a color I've never seen before. It's silver but with a glowing sheen that lightens the greenness in his skin, making it seem brighter around the tattoos. They fit him so well.

Kano looks down at his chest and smiles, "They're life-bond markings, *ĝhajo* markings. It means both of my hearts beat now that I have found my *ĝha*."

"Both hearts?" I ask, looking up to meet his eyes.

He pulls my hands to his chest, resting them above the tattoos, and I can feel the *thud-thud* of each heart beneath his skin. My eyes widen in surprise. The hearts beat in tandem, like that is what was always intended. *Two hearts.*

"Incredible," I whisper, leaning my ear against his chest. His hand brushes down my hair as he leans in to kiss me.

This isn't like before, when we were so eager to touch each other that we could hardly get home. No. This moment is special. When my lips meet Kano's, I accept this bond we share. I hear what the marks genuinely mean to him. I feel their effects in my own body, and I want them. The pure, unadulterated love is warm and languid in my blood. His heartbeat matches up with mine, and everything feels right. My desire is renewed.

Kano lifts me from the ground, bridal style, carrying me into our room. Thin curtains are drawn around the colored windows, blocking out the moons' light outside, but I can still see Kano's eyes in the dark. He lays me on the bed like I'm made of porcelain and ever so slowly kisses up my body. A teasing kiss placed on my calf, my thigh, right below my belly button. He moves up my body, between my breasts, along my neck, and the palm of my hand. Then, he kisses my face, cheek, forehead, and lips.

I sighed into him, melting into the mattress beneath me. The pillowy bed dips beneath his weight, and he moves forward, placing his throbbing cock at my entrance. He pauses, looming over me like this to peek at my face. My nerves flare, seeing Kano's cock pressed up against me. I'm wetter than I've ever been, but he's bigger than anyone I've ever been with.

"Are you ready, My Soul?"

He's so earnest, I nod. My hands come to his sides, gripping his thick skin. I lean my head back and try to relax. So, so slowly, he pushes into me, filling me in a way I've never experienced. It's pleasure with an edge of pain. And it feels so, so right. He thrusts himself forward, and I whimper. He stops immediately, looking down at my face with concern.

I glance between our bodies and groan. Kano is still inches from being able to fit inside me, but I want him. I want it. In his stillness, my body adjusts, and my desire deepens. With a deep breath, I nod.

"Keep going," I order, though my tone is weak. Kano shuttles forward another inch before I tense around him, biting back another whimper. This time, Kano doesn't stop.

He pauses for only a moment, curling down to kiss the top of my head before pressing forward again, growling, "You can take it, My Vera."

And I do. He slides in until my clit rubs against the studded patch of skin above his cock. Sensations skitter through me, releasing the tension in my muscles.

"Do you feel me, My Vera?" He asks as he draws out halfway before thrusting back in hard. It's like I can only feel him. All of me is focused on the slide of his cock in and out of me. Every thrust drags across my g-spot and stimulates my clit, keeping me connected to him – mind, body, and soul.

"Mhmm," I hum. He thrusts inside me again, rubbing a thumb across my bare nipple, "Yes."

My arousal grows until a babble of sounds comes from me. Moans, gasps, pleas of 'yes,' and more tumble from my lips. Kano meets me sound for sound. Each time he fills me completely, he grunts his own words of approval.

Thrust. "Yes, My Vera. You look so beautiful, stuffed with my cock."

His eyes flash from where our bodies meet to my face, watching it twist with pleasure. I can feel myself grow wetter as the filthy sounds of him inside me echo around the room. My head tilts back, my eyes squeezing closed from the pleasure. He brushes his thumbs across my nipples, tugging them gently.

Thrust. "So responsive."

I feel him tense above me, and his pace quickens slightly. Thrust. Thrust. Thrust. "Look at me."

My eyes flash open, meeting his in the dimness of the room. The intensity in his gaze is enough to send me over the edge, but Kano does nothing by half.

He grunts, "Come for me, my heart."

My lips part as my body bends to his command. I spasm around him, shouting his name. His tattoos flash, and he stills. My name is a prayer on his lips as I feel the first splash of his cum inside me. Rotating my hips against him, I wring pleasure from us both until we're sated.

We both lie still as we try to catch our breath. Then, Kano tugs me to his chest, letting his cock slide out of me and rolling onto his back. He drags one of the light sheets over us with a single arm and holds me against him sleepily.

His voice is rough when he whispers, "I love you, My Vera."

I freeze at his words, pretending I did not hear them. Then, as romantic as his desire to have me near him, I give him three minutes before I try to detangle myself from his arms. An infection on a foreign planet is the last thing I need, and I need an inch of space to process his words.

"Stay," He murmurs, holding me to him tighter.

"I have to pee," I respond, straining against him. He lets go of me but begrudgingly. And only after I promise to come straight back. Which I do. After my body is taken care of, I crawl right back on top of my prominent alien leader and have the best night's sleep of my life.

CHAPTER THIRTY-FIVE

It pains me to leave my *ĝha* after she accepted me as hers. But I must. Climbing from the bed, I quietly get ready for the day, glancing back at my sleeping *ĝha* once more before I leave. My Vera is beautiful when she sleeps. In her sleep, she does not hide her emotions from me. Her brows furrow when she dreams of her time before Wupeso. And when she has a good dream, a small smile will tilt her pink lips. Her lips are tilted in a smile. I kiss her forehead before walking out the door, praying to the Baso Sheva that My Vera sleeps peacefully until I return. I do not want to leave her. But unfortunately, another human woman demands my attention.

The fire-headed Az-ton stands outside with her arms crossed over her chest and a look of distaste. The air is chilled without the sun in the sky, and I wish for the warmth of my *ĝha*, under my sheets once more. Yet, here I am, determined to win the heart of My Heart's gatekeeper.

"Kano," she says in greeting, eyeing me as if I am a creature of the chasm.

"Az-ton," I reply, glancing back at my home. I wonder if it is too late to return to my *ĝha* and spend the day in our bed.

Az-ton interrupts my thoughts with, "Are you going to show me the place, or what?"

I can tell the human female Az-ton is upset, but I do not press. Instead, I focus on the bonding we are here to do.

"It is this way, Az-ton. We will meet Lewe at the field's edge."

Together, we walk north toward the field of wild *hazhiruga*. The sun is still a sliver from rising, but Az-ton does not complain of the darkness or terrain. When I look back to check on her, she waves me forward.

"My dad was a big hiker," She explains as if I know what a hiker is or why her father being one has any bearing on her ability to navigate the trail in the darkness.

It does not take long to reach the point where the fields meet the cliffs, and Lewe waits. Unlike Royi and Rihu's mounts, Lewe does not like the floating island near the *peholoe* loft. Even as a hatchling, he was a gentler creature than others of his kind. He preferred the smell of the fresh flowers and the splash of the heated pool. Which is why his nest is below the cliffside and why my home is so close to the *hazhiruga.*

I whistle for Lewe, and he comes shooting over the cliff's edge, landing beside us and dredging pollen with his wings. Lewe is rather large for a mount, but he's gentle and kind with strangers. Still, Az-ton takes two steps back.

"We really have to fly?" She asks, eyeing Lewe with distaste. My Vera mentioned Az-ton's fear of heights, but I know she has flown with Royi and Rihu. Llazho was more than happy to tell me all about their tactics to woo his *ĝha.*

"Yes. It is easiest, Az-ton."

"Easiest and must-do are two entirely different things." She says, eyeing Lewe warily. The place we are going would take multiple days of travel if we did not fly. By ship, it takes the lachyasugo numerous days to reach the mere shade of it. By flight, it only takes mere slivers of the sun. So flying is the most logical choice.

"You have flown with Royi and Rihu," I huff, latching the harness to my mount. Lewe lowers his head to make it easier, ruffling his feathers and perching low for easy access. I pat his head because he is the very best mount.

"Rihu and Royi gave me no choice," She grumbles, pacing back and forth across from me. "It seems to be a theme here."

"The V`òllø people only wish to do what is best for you," I explain, checking all the straps once again. When they are finished, I motion for her to climb on and offer a hand.

"Clearly not. Only Llazho can tell me what's best for me."

I want to agree with her. A person's *ĝha* has an inner knowing of what their *ĝha* may need, especially early in its activation. The only person who may know better than one's *ĝha* is oneself. But her tone of voice seems off to me. I am not sure she is serious with her words. So, I stay silent, latching her into the harness.

Climbing up behind her, Lewe takes flight. The sun's light begins to break the early sky, bathing the water beneath us in a warm glow. Clouds drift across the sky, flat and long and scattered. Az-ton is silent and grouchy, though this was her idea, and it makes me long to spend time with my *ĝha* once again. I wonder if My Vera is awake or if she still dreams of happy experiences. I wonder if she will be pleased with what Az-ton has planned for her. Or that Az-ton and I will be friends.

"Is that it?" She calls over the wind, her voice loose and frayed from her fear and lack of *jisa*. I tilt my horns to the side, and Lewe circles the edge of the floating island. It is the place that has hard, shiny rocks of many colors. And the thin, waxy leaves that are good for record-keeping. Az-ton says they are suitable for an "engagement gift."

Lewe lands along the edge, walking into a clearing to deposit us on the island. I am instantly on alert. The island may hold many shiny stones that might appeal to human women, but it also contains many different hunting beasts with claws sharp enough to take down a V`òllø woman. So, it will be important that Az-ton and I stick to the trails and keep our business here quick.

"We're looking for a diamond and about fifty-two of those waxy leaves you mentioned."

"The hard, clear stones?" I ask, scanning the ground. Crystals and gems are abundant on this island, existing in even the soil as if they had grown there. Many are hard and chippable and make for sharp weaponry, while others are more crystalline and fragile, like those in the crystal fields.

"Yep," Az-ton bends down to pull a gem from the ground. It is not as hard nor clear, but instead, it is a milky white color with lines of iridescent reds, pinks, and blues striped through it. She sighs deeply, dropping it back in the dirt before continuing onward. She does this many times. She will sigh in many ways – wistful sighs, annoyed sighs, thoughtful sighs. Then, she will drop the item she holds and continue on the trail. It makes me uncomfortable.

"Is something wrong?" I finally ask, after her tenth sigh since the light of the island's edge faded.

She stops in her tracks, coming to sit on a rock glittering with gems. She leans in on herself, dropping her head to her hands with a rough sob. Her eye-rain begins, and I take a step back. So many of the human women had eye-rain when they arrived. They were scared of their displacement and fearful of my people. At the welcome dinner, one woman cried even through the meal. My Vera told me this eye rain was called tears, though nothing tears when it happens.

Az-ton sobs, a muffled, "Everything is wrong."

My discomfort grows, but I feel myself ask, "Why?"

Her eyes are red, puffy, and watery when she looks back at me, and I do my best to control my reaction. Az-ton, a normally fine human, looks almost monstrous with the changes these tears have made to her face. She snorts.

"It's called ugly crying. Look it up."

I glance at the sky, asking the Baso Sheva for direction, but that only makes Az-ton laugh, then sob harder. She sniffles wetly, brushing away rivers of tears with the back of her hand.

"Here you are, making this big effort for Vera, who is such a simple person to please. But seriously, she doesn't even need all this. You're finding her a stone for a wedding ring because I told you to, not because she asked. You gather waxy leaves for her cards because I told you to, not because she asked. And she's going to love the gifts, trust me. But Vera doesn't need these things to feel loved. If you treat her with a modicum of respect, she will go to war for you. I know because she's my best friend. She's amazing."

Az-ton shouts her words, putting emphasis on her love for my *ĝha*. Then, her voice quiets, and she continues, tears cutting marks in the redness of her face, "And I'm happy for her. I swear. I even like Wupeso. But me? The girl who does care about these things. Who would want a human wedding and misses her family on Earth and loves gifts, quality time, and acts of service, gets Llazho."

Her hands slap against her legs with irritation, and she angrily brushes her tears away. Her moods fly from one intensity to another so quickly I have no choice but to stand still and listen, trying to find the connection between her words. Then, as I am about to tell her of Llazho's virtues, she proceeds.

"He doesn't do nice things for me, ask me about myself, or try to make friends with my best friend. He shows up with his know-it-all attitude and tells me what to do. I've managed so far, haven't I? It's infuriating."

"You should tell him what you want," I offer, choosing again to keep my distance.

"I try! I told him to leave me alone and that there wasn't anything going on between Rihu and Royi and me, but *they* brought me gifts and asked me questions about myself. So, of course, I'm friendly. I'm a nice person, and I need friends who won't tell me what the fuck I should be doing in the worst phase of my life. Sorry."

"Why do you apologize?" My confusion about the situation gets worse. There are many things I do not understand about Az-ton, like how she fights with her *ĝha* though she does not know him. Or why she recommended we get shiny rocks for My Vera, even though it is really her that wants them. Or why she apologizes for undisclosed reasons.

"Oh, Vera doesn't like it when I curse. She says it's a surefire way to stay pissed off," Az-ton picks up a shiny, clear stone off the ground, "She's probably right."

"My Vera is very wise," I agree, though I still do not understand why she would apologize to me for such words.

Az-ton hands me the clear stone. "That should be a good one. Now we have to get the leaves."

Az-ton knows my *ĝha* well. I inspect the stone thoroughly, enjoying the clarity and edges. It is a beautiful gem. Moreover, it will look fantastic adorning the hand of my *ĝha*. I tilt my head with approval, and we start on our way back.

Together, we collect the leaves along the trail. The shiny rock Az-ton liked still sits in the brush on the way back, and I pick it up, quietly tucking it in my pocket. Az-ton may not know how to talk to Llazho about what she wants, but he will listen to me. If this stone will help him win his *ĝha*, then it is an easy thing for me to pick it up. And if happiness with her own *ĝha* will make Az-ton happy, it will make Vera happy, which makes me happy.

It was a good outing. With a few more than fifty-two leaves and an engagement stone in my pocket, we return to the home island, where my *ĝha* waits for me.

CHAPTER THIRTY-SIX

Apparently, it's too much to ask, waking up beside the person you had sex with the night before, even on Shojo. This is why I try to rage-bake some form of pancakes over an open flame beside the world's worst allergen. And where's your best friend when you need her? She is probably asleep in the *peholoe* loft dreaming about crushing human men's hearts for not saving her from this planet because she hates her "soulmate."

Gamble away your two percent chance of leaving; why don't you? Take a chance on alien love; it'll be fun, you said. Sleep with the hot V`òllø guy who worships the ground you walk on, right?

"No, not right, Vera. He'll up and leave you like any other fu —"

"Vee!" Aston calls, running down the soft slope of the hill. I snap my mouth shut, forcing myself to smile as I flip my pancake. She looks like she's been crying, but she grins like a loon. Her hair is all windswept and wild, and her eyes are puffier than usual. She glances at my morning meal and her brow creases. She knows what pancakes mean. Just because this batter is green and this pancake is burnt doesn't change the facts. Aston's face falls, "What happened?"

Rage burns inside me. "I'll tell you what happened, I decided to fornicate with the alien king, and he decided he couldn't be bothered for some morning cuddles."

I hear the pan sizzle behind me and twist away from Aston to flip another burnt pancake. Pulling the first pancake off, I try a bite before tossing it straight into the fire. Note to self, just because it looks like flour doesn't mean it tastes like flour. The gritty, grassy taste envelops my tongue, and I force myself to swallow.

Turning back to Aston, I see her face has paled.

I snap, "What?"

"You guys had sex last night?"

"Uh, yeah. Did you not see how we were practically grinding on each other after that game of Neked'I? If those kids hadn't smacked him in the face with their frisbee, we might've done it in town."

"Well, shit."

"Language." My head begins to ache in a way only pancakes can soothe.

"Vee, don't be mad at Kano."

"I'll be mad at Kano if I want. What kind of big alien doofus thinks he can give me multiple O's and bail before the sun? It wasn't even light out when I woke up." I dump the rest of the batter into the pot, thinking maybe the kids will eat it if it looks like cake.

Aston squeaks, "Oh, no."

Then, big arms wrap around me tight, and his hot breath is against my ear.

"I missed you, My Vera."

I don't want to stop being angry, but it's like someone pulled the plug, and my anger spirals down the drain. With Kano's arms around me and his kind words in my ear, I want to melt. But I was mad. He was gone this morning. Not a word or a sleepy kiss. As much as I hate to do it, I pull myself from his arms. Ducking below his elbow and stepping away.

"Where were you this morning?" I cross my arms over my chest to communicate my anger. Aston shakes her head behind him, crossing her hand over her throat like I should stop, but I'm not that difficult to please. All he has to do is respect me a little bit, and not even my apparent soulmate can manage.

"Aston and I —"

"Excuse me? Rather than being in bed with me, you went off with my best friend before the sun rose? To where? To do what, Kano? Choose your words carefully."

Aston facepalms behind him, and I glare in her direction. I knew she was struggling to adjust on this planet, but surely she didn't need to steal Kano from my bed right after we had sex. And Kano? Was I so naïve as to believe a stranger about being his soulmate? He was probably working his way through all the human women. Fury lashes through me at the thought. If he thought he could belong to anyone else, he was wrong. We had a deal. Kano is mine.

I feel murderous rage and possessiveness flaring through me. Some logical part of my brain reminds me that Aston is my best friend, and I've known her forever, and she would never do the images my mind concocts, but it's too late.

"It's a surprise," Kano tells me, and I dump my unfinished pancake cake into the fire, whirling on the traitors. 'Surprise' could mean any number of ludicrous things, but my mind refuses to see reason.

"Time to make some things clear," I start, stalking toward them. Aston is at least smart enough to take a step back, remembering when I turned this fury on her older brother for belittling her life's work. Unfortunately, Kano is ever clueless about the power of my wrath.

"Kano, you are mine."

The truth flares through me, and I wonder if lightning strikes me from the inside out. The skin above my heart burns, and I grit my teeth against the pain. Then, the same shimmer surrounding Kano bubbles around me, dancing across my skin. I can see it shake over my fingers and down my palm. I'm so surprised that Aston takes the chance to sputter out an explanation.

"Before last night's festival, I told Kano you would want a wedding ring. You never thought you'd get one on Earth because you only fell for losers and deviants. I told him about diamonds, and he knew a place we could get you one. So, we made plans to go this morning before you ever slept together."

As if finally understanding that I was mad at him, Kano immediately drops to his knees before me and explains further, pulling the rock from his pocket, "It is for your engagement gift. A romantic human custom."

The diamond is huge but not outrageous. It is also clear and naturally smooth on one side. All my rage at my *ĝha* and friend dissipates. The edges of my possessiveness smooth over. They were thinking about making me happy. They were going above and beyond. Kano didn't know about customary morning cuddles and wanted to surprise me with an engagement ring.

"My Vera, I promise I didn't want to leave you. I was the most blessed of men to have you in my arms. Leaving you was like pulling my hearts out of my chest," He admits when I take the rock from his hand. It's not a ring yet, but I'm sure they have a plan for that too. I hold it against my finger. Much bigger than I would have got on Earth, for sure.

But something still isn't adding up.

"When did you two become such great friends?"

They answer in unison.

Aston says, "We're not."

While Kano replies, "Aston means a lot to you, so she means a lot to me."

Kano is surprised by Aston's answer; that much is clear. But Aston's face says it all. She cried this morning, probably spilling her guts to Kano. She would never admit to becoming his friend, but the words he said this morning supported her, and the beginnings of friendship were blossoming. And I couldn't be more grateful.

CHAPTER THIRTY-SEVEN

Hoga, one of the *peholoe,* was not one to be trifled with. The batty woman had me wait for an entire sliver of the sun, of which I'd learned there are twenty-two before the nighttime even began. Days and weeks were longer here, and with Blossom's explanation of the V`òllø calendar, time started to make sense. For example, the reason my sleep was all over the place was because of the extended sunlight hours.

One thing Blossom wasn't able to explain was the shimmering second skin I'd achieved in my fight with Kano. Or the tattoo across the top of my left breast that matched his. The so-called intelligence referred me to one Miss Hoga for those questions. This is how I found myself waiting beside a garden bed at the bottom of the karst as the old woman hummed a gentle tune to a vegetable sprout.

"Are you going to just stare? Or are you going to help?" She finally asked, after letting me stand there, waiting away my last hours as a single human woman.

Huffing, I join her in the garden bed, propping up the burgeoning vegetable sprouts and gently placing them on the stick trellises. These plants look almost like green beans, but a swirling pattern of pink sets them apart from any food on Earth. They also seemed to live. As I'd pick one from the dirt and lay it near the trellis, it appeared to reach for the stick and curl itself around it. After all the little sprouts were propped up, Hoga pulled these invasive blue-grey plants from the root. They were sticky and spindly. The goo heated against my newfound shimmer. A realization Hoga noted.

By the end of the hour, Hoga watched me work. I pulled the weird weeds, propped bean sprouts, and used her little watering can to fill the tiny indents surrounding the bushes. I brushed the sweat from my brow and glanced back at her. She sat on the bottom step of the karst, staring in my direction.

"You look good with your *jisa*," she finally says to break the silence. I pop a squat by my current patch of weeds.

"And a *jisa* is?"

I will never get used to Hoga's smug smirk. She obviously knows why I'm here and what I need to know.

"The *shimmer,* as you have been calling it. It is your *jisa* or, rather, in your case, an extension of your *ĝha*'s *jisa*."

"Great, and what does this *jisa* do?" I curl my hands over my eyes to block out the sun as I stare at the *peholoe*. Hoga looks ethereal in this light. You might think she was an angel if you didn't know her temperament.

"Well, it protects from poison, like the toxin on those weeds," She explains, picking up a single one of the spindly plants.

"And it urges growth," She demonstrates again by curling one of the little bean sprouts around a trellis. My eyes widen a bit as the plant curls around the stick.

"But the best part," Hoga begins, a genuine smile on her face, "Is that it connects you to your *ĝha*."

I watch in surprise, and Hoga closes her eyes, tilting her head toward the sun. Her *jisa* glows brighter momentarily before dying to the dull shine against her skin again. Her smile falters, but she doesn't explain. She knocks her horns to both sides and urges me to try.

Standing like she did, I close my eyes, and Kano's jade eyes immediately glow back at me. Unlike human eyes but equally beautiful, I'm not as jarred to see these as I was the first time. It seemed some memory of him would be what I would see when my eyes closed for the rest of my life. Still, I didn't expect to hear some disembodied version of him in my mind. It was like writing on a page, but it was read in my memory of his voice.

"Why hello there, My Vera."

"You can hear me?"

"Well, you are reaching through the jisa.*"*

I open my eyes, finding myself standing exactly where I had been. The breeze off the bay rustled through my hair, pushing it over my shoulders. The late afternoon sun was still high in the sky. Half my body stood in its light, while the other half was protected by the shade of the karst. The shimmer on my skin glowed like crazy but slowly faded to its usual luminosity. I glanced down my tunic at the tattoo on my chest, and it seemed to be the same light color. It was slightly raised like a scar, but some inhuman ink stained the center of the pink ridges.

A twinge in my head forced my eyes closed, and Kano was in my mind.

"See, you reach through."

The pain faded immediately after, and I gave him a proper mental goodbye this time.

It felt incredible and terrifying. I couldn't understand the magic behind it or the science if this could be explained that way. It didn't feel real, even though I'd experienced it. Part of me wondered if I had died on that spacecraft. Was this the afterlife I had landed in? I look over to Hoga, waiting on the steps.

If so, it's definitely not heaven.

"It's incredible," I finally admit to her, trying to overlook her sad smile. Hoga pats the step beside her, and I join her in that seat. She grabs my hand in hers and closes her eyes. I follow her lead. Then, I feel it.

Lost somewhere in this energy field, I can feel Kano's soul. It's strong and vibrant, and attractive. I can feel myself waver toward it, but there seems to be a wall between us. He exists in a different space than I share with Hoga now. No, this space is dull. A slight vibration of pain, tolerable but present, works through us. We share it as if it's a load we can both carry. And in the weight, if you're searching for it, you can feel the weak pull of several different *jisa*. A masculine tone, a feminine note, a myriad of essences coagulate and liquefy. I can feel Hoga's energy, bright like my own, beside me. It reaches for that masculine tone and seems to hum in harmony when it meets it.

Then, our eyes are opened again, and we're pulled back to the present. The mounts caw overhead, and the hollow sound of the breeze against the karst echoes around us. We can smell the scent of the dirt and the floral smell of festival garland. The light breeze washes away the remaining energy, and Hoga returns to her usual closed demeanor.

"You understand."

It's not a question, so I don't answer with words. I simply squeeze her hand and sit with her in silence.

CHAPTER THIRTY-EIGHT

"Surprise!" Everyone shouts. I jump practically to the roof, feeling my *jisa* snap out to protect me from fear. Zhalisee and Aston stand with huge grins on their faces. They have gathered all the women in the village (and Pa) to the *peholoe* loft tonight, and it's dripping in decorations. A pot of flowers sits on the center of the table, and garlands are draped along the inner walls, woven through the outer slats. The mat where Hoga and I play Neked'I has been moved out of the way, and Blossom plays familiar music from her speakers.

I thought it was weird when Hoga demanded I walk her to the loft, but after the tender moment we shared, I figured she didn't want to be alone. From the lack of surprise on her face, I have a feeling she knew about this. Hoga played a surprise party decoy, and that brought a smile to my face.

"What is all this for?" I ask, motioning to the room. They've done an incredible job setting up some kind of party, but it's not my birthday, so I can't figure it out.

"Bachelorette Party. According to my calculations, your wedding is tomorrow," Aston says. Hoga and Blossom both confirm her words.

"You didn't have to do all this." Plates and plates of food are piled along the table, making that floral centerpiece stand out. Gifts are wrapped in swaths of fabric, and all the little floor cushions are arranged in a circle. Blossom is bobbing her head along to the music she plays, and all the *peholoe* are present, standing awkwardly among the human women, with their horns slightly tilted down.

"We haven't done anything yet," Aston says, pulling me away from Hoga and to the circle of seats. She places me at the front of the room, and all the women (and Pa), gather around. Standing at the circle's center, I watch my best friend shine. "On Earth, the planet we came from, a bachelorette party is a rite of passage. It is a way for women to celebrate their final night as a free and single, unmated person."

Aston goes around the room, placing flower crowns on everyone's heads, winding them carefully over horns, and declaring them party people. Then, she sets the biggest one on my head, and a gem dangles from the front.

"Now, I've curated some of the best bachelorette party activities for us to enjoy this evening. As newly minted party people, there are some rules. And you live by these rules until the sun rises in the morning!"

She goes on to hype up the women (and Pa) with her rules of enjoyment, having a good time, and keeping an open mind for her list of activities. Then, the *tsare* comes out, and a round of truth, dare, or drink begins.

"Truth or drink?" Roxie asks, cheeks the color of a tomato. Aston wanted everyone to have a turn to ask someone a question before we moved on to the next game, but Roxie had been receiving an unfair number of requests, many of which were concerning her and Kethi. Roxie only ever responded to those questions with a drink. Luckily, it was finally her turn to twist the table.

"Truth," I say, leaving my glass of *tsare* untouched. So far, I'd bared the tattoo on my tit, told them the approximate size of Kano's penis, and shared the story of my lucky cards. Games were my safe place to let my competitive side free. Truth, dare, or drink was no different. If rising to the challenge was how someone won this game, I would rise to every challenge.

Roxie hiccups, blinking her sleepy eyes before asking, "Do you love him?"

The party people ooh, as if this is some big, juicy secret, and maybe it is. I give myself a moment to think about it, toying with my glass of *tsare*. The room is leaning on a ledge, captivated by my thoughts. *Do I love him?*

Kano was tall and handsome, even in his strange way. We had great sex, but it was more than that. Kano chose me the moment he saw me. He pursued me wholeheartedly. He knew that I existed before our arrival, though he had no reason to. He saved me when I ran off to do something stupid, and he didn't expect anything in return. He's respectful to me and to everyone around him. He gave me space when I first arrived, even though it probably killed him to do it. He never forced himself on me, only chasing after me to ensure I was okay. Then, he went out of his way to befriend my friend because he knew it was important to me. But could I really love him?

Yeah. Yes, I did love Kano. It was the warm feeling in my chest when he was around and the possessiveness I felt when he gave others his attention. My love was evident in how my edges smoothed around him and how I hated being apart. It was prominent in the mornings we woke up together and the *jisa* we both shared. I loved Kano, but I wasn't about to admit that to a room full of women before he heard it from my lips.

So, I took a sip of my *tsare* and forfeited the game.

ston really went above and beyond with the party.
When Roxie started slurring, Aston called truth or
drink, and we all ended up eating away at the prepared
feast to dampen the effects of the alcohol. With food in our
bellies and the ice broken between everyone, it was time for
the next event.

It seemed everyone in attendance had brought me some
kind of gift. The human women gifted me little things based on
Earth items they thought I would appreciate. Cerridwen
knitted me a pillow with some sticks and feathers Zhu
provided her. Daria made a bracelet from my old shirt. Roxie
even tested her craft skills to make me linen pasties in the
shapes of stars for my honeymoon. The V`òllø women did a
fantastic job too. They provided me things I might need for my
household, cleaning supplies, storage containers, and extra
clothes. But my favorite gift was from Aston. That morning she
stole Kano from me was not for nothing. Bright green cards
have been cut from leaves and dried around the edges. The
suits are drawn on and numbered out, creating a full deck of
cards.

"Ace, this is —"

"Amazing? Brilliant? Perfect? I know. But the best gift
has yet to come."

I heard the caw of the crow-things outside, and then
Rihu and Royi came sauntering into the loft. Blossom switches
the music from nondescript dance beats to sexy R&B hits.

And that is how we found ourselves watching alien
strippers.

The human women are living for it, laughing and
sharing their wish for dollar bills, but the alien women are the
ones who really make it a party. They whoop and holler and
dance with each other as Rihu and Royi make complete fools
of themselves. Aston claps in tune with the beat, cheering as

they take off their shirts. Even Daria is in on it, calling for them to keep stripping. To which they oblige without question.

When they're down to nothing but a caveman loincloth, Aston redirects them to dancing with the women. It reminds me of the last night on the ship before everything went sideways. Aston and I had danced until our feet ached. Only this time, when I woke up the following day, I was pretty confident I wouldn't be facing the lousy kind of stranded in space.

The party died down about halfway through the night. Blossom said she needed to recharge, and the women found places to crash. It didn't escape my notice that Pa and Alba slunk off together or that Roxie slipped out of the loft. Aston had done a great job with the party, and she was mentally preparing to clean up when I told her to go to bed. Ace fought me a little before I told her it would take me some time to wind down after all the fun, and the cleaning would help. She knew it was true, so she released the dirty dish and disappeared from the living area.

I worked alone for a while, consolidating food dishes into one big bowl and walking it over to the chest of ice crystals. Then, I washed the plates under the running water with the spongey plants Zhalisee taught me about. Finally finished with the dishes, I start washing down the table, making sure to leave the beautiful flowers they put together.

Hoga emerges from the shadows like a wraith, criticizing, "You don't wash the table with those. It scratches the grain."

"Then what do I wash the counters with?"

"A cloth," She replies as if I'm the stupid one. In the week I've been here, I haven't been taught a single thing about survival. Kano has made sure every one of my needs has been met. With the help of other men and the *peholoe*, this had been the truth for many human women. Still, I listen to her now. Pulling a cloth from the directed place, I put it in the salve she recommends and wipe it over the table.

As usual, Hoga watches me work in silence. She doesn't say anything unless it's to correct me, which means she doesn't say anything. Then, when the table is clean, the fabric from the gifts is folded up, and the cushions are rearranged to their proper places, Hoga pulls out the Neked'I mat and begins a game.

I sit across from her without a word. We go back and forth, shifting around our chips and focusing on our strategies. She speaks only when we're about halfway through our game.

"Are you ready for tomorrow?" She moves an infinite chip to her circle, glancing over at my play space. Over the many games I've lost to her, I've learned keeping an eye on your opponent helps.

"I mean, I have no idea what to expect, but yes."

"Well, Az-ton has told me much of human *wed-dings,* and a *R ̈uṣad'ù* is not the same," Hoga says, observing me. I'm about three moves from winning, but I'm sure Hoga has a strategy to stop me.

"Then, why don't you tell me?"

"Now you have asked," She states, moving another set of her chips. "*R ̈uṣad'ù* is a memorable ceremony in our culture. It requires both parties to perceive one another fully. To enter into the darkness alone and come out together."

"Hoga, I'm too tired for riddles. Can you just spell it out for me? Give me the skinny? Explain in simple terms."

188

She takes her turn in the game, sighing deeply. "There is a cave beyond the crystals you will enter, blindfolded. Kano will already be there, with only the direction of his third eye and the connection from your *jisa*. You must come out of the cave together to be blessed by the Baso Sheva. Those who enter but do not exit together are cursed. Those who enter but do not exit at all are presumed dead."

I'm about to lay my winning chip, but my hands still.

"Are you saying there is a chance I don't survive my wedding?"

"You must truly love Kano if you plan to go through with the *r ̈uṣad'ù* because he is our leader, and he will not leave that cave without you."

I finish laying my chip, but the feeling of winning is lost on me. Hoga doesn't believe I love him. Shame from not admitting my feelings to the women earlier in the evening and denying how I feel about Kano even a little fills me. I meet Hoga's eyes.

"Kano and I will come out of that cave together tomorrow."

Her eyes flash, and her genuine smile, which I've only seen a handful of times, lights her face. Then, she says, "Good, because you and the human women are fighters. And I could tell from the moment you stepped onto Wupeson soil that you are the kind to win."

CHAPTER THIRTY-NINE

The sun has not yet risen when I begin my prayers. Kneeling in the crystal shards, I bow my horns low to the Baso Sheva. Today, this choice to practice faith weighs on me. I have not seen my *ĝha* in hours, and an unfamiliar sense of doubt weighs on my horns. I feel as if everything has happened too easily. My *ĝha* was nervous about me initially, but I listened to my elders and trusted the Baso Sheva, and she accepted me in her bed. She agreed to join me in the *r̈uṣad'ù*. But she has not spoken 'I love you' to me as I have her.

Though she has promised to stay here with me, I fear that she does not love me the way I love her. My Vera is caring. She loves her friends, the human women, but especially Az-ton. My *ĝha* is strong of mind. She adapted to our home quickly, efficiently handling each new obstacle thrown at her. She doesn't mind taking risks and challenges me to think outside the prescribed method. Since her arrival, my faith has been stronger. Since she began staying in my home, my devotion to our people has grown. Since she willingly shared her body with me, I've wanted only her love.

In answer to my prayers of fear, I hear Baso Sheva's words. *Fear is derived from a lack of faith.*

So, I release my fear to the Baso Sheva. I trust that my *ĝha* will make mention of her love. I trust that we will succeed in our *r̈uṣad'ù* together. Most of all, I trust Baso Sheva.

CHAPTER FORTY

Turns out my wedding dress is blue.

I wasn't the kind of girl who really dreamed about some big princess wedding with the fluffy white dress and the picket fence dreams attached. I came from a poor side of town, and my family was full of addicts. So I didn't have any big illusions about the kind of money I would have or marry into. And I didn't have the time to daydream about what my wedding would look like or curate a pinboard. I didn't expect a blue dress, though.

It wasn't the usual linen fabric we used for our day-to-day wear here in Wupeso. Instead, it was silky and light, draping across my body like a liquid sky. Well, earth sky. Tiny blue gems had been hand-stitched into the bodice at various intervals, and the dress fit me like a glove.

Hoga hated it.

"It's not traditional," She huffs. Little did I know I wouldn't please everyone, even on Shojo. Aston gears up to defend my dress choice – which she made. Then, I step in and grab Hoga's horns.

"Don't you think marrying a human is nontraditional?"

The *peholoe* keeps her feelings to herself, holding out the cream blindfold I'll wear before entering the cave. Aston snatches it from her hands defensively, and I can't help but smile a little. Even on a different planet, Aston is determined to prove her mettle.

"You ready?" She asks, taking a final glance over my wedding look. Boots and an overly beautiful gown, flowers and crystals in my hair, homemade makeup, and a soft updo made me look like a proper bride for an alien. But that wasn't what she was really asking.

"I'm ready."

"Good," Aston takes my arm, leading me down the karst and back up the hill toward the crystal fields.

Many of the Vˋòllø people wave to us on the way, taking their time singing and skipping along the track. The few kids in the village dart between legs, chasing some *ŝœhů̥*. Music is played on stringed instruments similar to guitars and tonal chimes that they smack against different surfaces. Part of me wishes to take my time like they do, but Aston rushes me along, pushing me toward the crystal fields.

When we reach the line of purple sand, she stops, looking over my outfit again and giving her approval.

"Okay, you know what to expect?" She asks, fidgeting with the petals of a flower in my hair.

"Pa and the chosen witnesses will watch me enter the cave. First, Pa will put on my blindfold and recite some prayers. Then, everyone will be invited to join as Kano and I navigate it and come out hand-in-hand."

"Yep. It's not exactly vows and cake, but we get what we get, right?" Aston's eyes shine, and I can tell she's moments from freaking out. So, I nod my agreement and hug her tight. As she's squeezed against me, she whispers, "And, so you know, your lucky cards are sewn into this little pouch."

Aston taps the side of my thigh, and I feel the box's corners smack my skin. The mere sweetness of the moment is not lost on me, but Aston doesn't dally or wait for my tearful thanks. Instead, she lets me squeeze her tighter.

My words are muffled against her, but no less critical, "I love you, Ace."

“I love you too, Vee.”

CHAPTER FORTY-ONE

This moment of standing in the darkness alone is probably unnerving for most. For me, it feels like the time before my *ĝha* arrived. I trust that she will show based on the same faith I held before her arrival. I trust that she will reach out to me through the *jisa.* I trust that we will make it out of the darkness together.

Tradition states I cannot use my third eye until she's entered the chambers. So, I wait until the whispered words of ritual are whispered through the walls. In the eye of the Baso Sheva, the cave looks different. What is ordinarily beautiful, silvery crystal walls now seem to buzz with a hundred different colors. Reds, blues, and yellows blend and slide against the crystalline structures. Even the floor appears to glitter; energy pulses from every angle.

Since my usual sight is blocked, it is easy to reach out through the *jisa,* searching for my *ĝha* and her spirit. She meets me in mind immediately, calling my name.

"Kano?"

"Yes, My Vera."

"How do I find you?"

"We find each other. Your jisa *should pull you in a certain direction. Follow it."*

"Okay."

Her mind detaches from mine, and I feel the pull on my *jisa.* My third eye can see it. The energy of my *jisa* is a very specific color. Green like my eyes, with an iridescent silver glow like my tattoos. It looks like smoke as it winds through the labyrinthine tunnels and toward my *ĝha.* Her footsteps echo throughout the chamber, distorting the sound of which direction she may be in. So, I rely on my third eye to guide me. I feel her tug against my *jisa* and answer immediately.

"I'm scared," she says, and I can feel her shake against the wall. I want to tell her that nothing in this cave is scary enough to fear and that the Baso Sheva is with us, but I know My Vera doesn't believe the same things I do. So, I try other words.

"I love you. I am with you. We will do this together."

I feel her stop, and I hear her footsteps fade. She disconnects.

My body still leads me to her, but my hearts feel bruised in my chest. My faith wavers as thoughts of her leaving me alone here infect my mind. My *jisa* is still strong, its waves of color guiding me through my third eye. But the doubt halts me in my tracks. Then, I feel her pull on the bond again.

"I love you, too. I wanted to tell you in person, but I didn't have time, and then the r̈u̥ṣad'ù was already here, and human and V`òllø tradition didn't allow it. We do this together, right?"

I hear her footsteps begin again, and my faith is renewed. My pull toward her strengthens, and my hearts beat stronger in my chest. The words from my ĝha's lips changed everything.

"Right, My Vera. Can you feel the pull?"

"Yes."

Together, in our minds, we navigate the caves without issue. Vera cannot see me without a third eye, so she jumps when my hands touch her shoulders. A small squeak echoes through the chamber, reverberating and appearing like stars in the sky.

"It's me, My Vera."

In the sight of my third eye, she is a vision. Our *jisa* shimmers over her body in the same green and silver waves of smoke, but beneath it, her life energy shines. Gold and red, it looks like magma. The beating of her heart is synced with mine. Her usually long, yellow hair is braided and pinned up from her neck, and the golden aura shines around her face.

"Can we remove the blindfolds now?" She asks, holding onto my wrist tightly.

I want to say yes, see her blue eyes in my third eye, and look directly into the contents of her soul. But I can't. Until we reach the mouth of the cave, we must stay blind to the dangers, of which there are still more to face.

"Not yet, My Vera."

"Okay," She murmurs softly, sliding her fingers through mine. She squeezes my hand gently, and I watch her aura's molten gold bend against mine. Then, together, we step toward the exit.

CHAPTER FORTY-TWO

Now that I'm with Kano, the wedding feels more approachable. When I arrived, Pa blindfolded me, leading me by the arm into the cave to my starting position. I couldn't see anything, and his whispered words made no sense without my earbud. After a moment, I could hear his footsteps trail away, echoing like music in the chamber. Immediately, I reached out for Kano, and I'd been thanking the stars or the goddess or whatever had existed on this planet since.

I squeeze his hand in mine, and he gives it a squeeze back. Then, he leads us out of the cave. The pull of my *jisa* is still strong, dragging me in the same direction we're heading, and I wonder if it's because the soul energy calls to the other V`òllø or the will of a higher power. His words are a warning in my ear, and that's when I realize I can understand him without my earbud.

"Tread carefully, My Vera. The floor is slick through here."

I pull us to a stop, "Wait, I can hear you."

Kano chuckles. "That is good, My Vera."

"No. No. I can hear you and *understand* you. I don't have my earbud."

I feel Kano's hand tilt my head to both sides before the vibration of joy reaches my body. "It must be our bond. The *ĝha* mark, maybe."

"So, you're saying if the other women accept their *ĝha*'s, they won't need the earbuds?"

"I suppose so," He replies, taking another step forward.

The floor is slick here, and even the grit-covered boots slip a little, sliding me into Kano. His skin feels like heaven on mine, and part of me wonders if we have time for a detour. But then, a sound like nails on a chalkboard scrapes and echoes through the chambers.

"What makes that sound?"

"Nothing you should concern yourself with, My Vera."

Still, he hurries me further along, letting me slide a bit to get over the tricky part of the cave. Through the blindfold, I figure we must be getting close to reaching the cave entrance because the darkness fades a little. But then it grows darker, and an unmistakable growl sends rancid, heated breath across my skin.

CHAPTER FORTY-THREE

Saliva drips from the fang of the *yue'e,* dripping to the floor and echoing through the chambers. Every bright and colorful wave of energy my third eye allows me to see is sucked into the blackness of the creature's aura. The smell of brimstone and rot invades the cramped space as the beast snarls in warning. Scales trail down its back as natural armor. Matte black, it moves like skin as the creature steps toward us. Its claws scrape and gouge the crystal floor. I push us both a step back, feeling the soft, breakable skin of my *ĝha* beneath my fingers.

I knew that every pair of *ĝhajo* that entered this cave faced a creature of some kind. Generally, the creatures were a conjuration of spirit, like an animal, dissipating at the lightest touch. *Ĝhajo* always faced the Baso Sheva's choice. I also knew that as the village's Rogeshu, I would likely face a complex beast. One made of real flesh and blood. However, I was not ready for a *yue'e.* The *yue'e* is an apex predator. Without my blindfold, it may have been a fair battle. With it, I fear we will be lucky to escape alive. With my *ĝha* beside me, I had no choice but to escape alive.

"What is it?" My *ĝha* whispers, her fingers shaking in mine.

"Something to concern yourself with, My Vera."

"What do we do?" She peers up at me. Though she cannot see my face, I try to keep the tension from it. A tendril of hair has fallen from her loose bindings, and I brush it behind her ear, keeping my eye on the beast blocking our exit.

"We are supposed to defeat it. Kill it."

"Is it big? It feels big."

"Yes, it is quite large."

"Do we have a weapon?"

It roars again, a wave of heat coming with it, and I search for an alternative exit. If the *yue'e* roars again, there is a good chance fire comes with it. My *jisa* can handle a lot, but the heat could consume me even if it were to block the flame. There is an alcove much closer to the beast, but if we use it to avoid the flame, we corner ourselves.

"Let's go this way," I say, trying to tug her by the hand back the way we came.

"But the exit is that way," She protests.

Her arm is flung out wide, and the *yue'e* looks like it has a mind to bite it from her body. Currently, it is waiting for us to make a move, and I have no intention of bringing it to action. I force her arm back to her side and search again for a weapon. A tiny pointy gem dangles against my *ĝha*'s forehead. It will have to do.

Flower petals tumble from her hair as I pull it from her head, and the beast chitters at the weapon in my hand. Sending up a prayer to the Baso Sheva, I decide I will defeat this beast for my *ĝha*.

"Good thinking," She whispers, keeping her hand in mine as we creep forward. A low growl rumbles along, and I release her hand, stepping in front of her. She stays one step behind me as I approach the beast. It hisses and growls, but we inch closer and closer. I'm preparing for a snarl of fire, ready to launch into action, when my *ĝha* grabs my shoulder.

I do not look away from the beast, but I tilt my head down for her words.

"Wait! What if he's hungry or hurt?"

Before I can assure her that is not the case, she slips from behind me and reaches out to touch the beast's steaming snout. I jump forward, ready to push my *ĝha* away from the beast's attack. But the beast stops growling, pressing its nose against Vera's hand. Its chittering turn to purring.

"Who's such a good beastie?" She coos as if speaking to a nursling. She runs the back of her hand over its thick snout and speaks to it gently. "What do you need, little beastie? Are you hungry?"

A huff comes from the beast, and Vera nods in agreement. "Of course you are. You've been trapped in a cave for some time."

The beast purrs against her hand again. "What about injuries? Are you hurt, baby?"

Jealousy rises in my chest at her kind words to the beast. Would she have cared for me this way if I were sick or injured? But the beast does not hurt My Vera. Instead, it nuzzles her hand and purrs against her chest, confirming it is not damaged. When I try to pull my *ĝha* away from the *yue'e*, it hisses in my direction. Its forked tongue slipped from its mouth in warning.

My Vera whispers, "Oh, c'mon. Play nice. If I have it my way, you and Kano must learn to get along."

Vera grabs my hand and places it on the beast's nose. Its jaws snap grouchily, but Vera's soft reprimands keep it from taking my hand. When the *yue'e* is comfortable, Vera explains how we need to exit the cave. She promises to come back with food for the *yue'e* and show it to its new home.

With a pitiful whine, the beast moves out of our way. Vera grabs my hand, and we move toward the exit. The sunlight is too bright to look upon with my third eye, so I close it as we step from the cave's darkness. My people cheer, and the blindfolds are removed from our faces. The human women whistle wildly to be heard over the V`òllø's cheers.

One of the women shouts, "Now you may kiss the bride!"

I look upon my mate with my natural vision for the first time since we exited the cave and survived our *r ̈uṣad'ù*. We are frazzled, but she is still the most beautiful woman I've ever seen. Her eyes shine with unshed tears, but she blinks them away, tilting her face up to see me.

"I love you," she says, and one of her tears falls away. "I wanted to tell you that earlier, but –"

I smash my lips to hers. The crowd cheers louder, but they are drowned out by the pure energy of my *ĝha*. Her hands come to rest in the crooks of my elbows, and a soft moan leaves her lips. My Vera pulls away from me, and I follow her lips, claiming them once again. She kisses me back for a moment longer before pulling away once again. I let her go this time, but only because the crowds' cheers have broken through the fog, and we must celebrate with my people.

CHAPTER FORTY-FOUR

I am exhausted by the time the celebrations have ended for the night. Dead on my feet, I drag a bucket of fresh meat through the sand to the crystal cave. Kano, my real-life alien husband, refused to come, saying he would meet me at home after he checked on his own beast. The guy didn't want to spend an hour apart only days ago. Now that we're married and I want to climb him like a tree, we can deal with our animals and meet up later. Earlier today, during our *r¨uṣad'ù*, I couldn't explain why I needed to comfort the creature. I had this prompting that it was the only way we would escape alive and that the animal had been delivered for me. Even in exhaustion, I was eager to set my eyes on it.

The cave was dark at this time of night, but that was all the better. It would be good for the creature to meet me in an open space without adjusting to the sunlight simultaneously.

I click my tongue and call for the creature, calling it *"Yue'e,"* as Kano did. My new pet doesn't take long to respond, carefully slinking out of the cave like the scaredy cat it is. Or rather, scaredy drake. The smell of brimstone comes with it as it walks closer to me.

"Wow," I whisper, my neck craning to see the beast as its head extends fully from its body. Twice the size of a horse, the drake looks like some kind of reptilian wolf. Instead of shifting fur, black scales move along its skin. I can remember the gritty feel of them under my fingertips. Four curling black horns decorate the top of its head. It has blood-red, slitted eyes and a matching underbelly. He sniffs the air beside me, probably smelling the meat I brought for him.

Presenting the food, I try to armor my voice with authority when I point at the ground and say, "Down."

The drake lies down and lets me slide the bowl over to him. He is obviously intelligent. He looks at me curiously, and I tell him eating is okay. Then, sitting cross-legged beside him, I speak kind words in a soft, gentle tone.

"Maybe Diablo. No, you look more like a Magnus. I think I'll call you Magnus. Does that seem okay?"

Magnus's eyes don't come up from his food, so I imagine he's OK with it. I run a hand down his neck while he eats and let myself rest on the sand. He takes his sweet time with the meat, so I post up against his side, closing my eyes for a minute. He is warm to the touch, if a little stinky. The gentle rising and falling of his chest as he breathes rock me gently. I can hear his heartbeat like thunder underneath his rough exterior. He doesn't jostle or snap at me when I lean against him, and the wind whistles through the crystals and makes a harmonic tune.

I wake with a start when Magnus growls, breaking me from my sleep on the sand. I don't know how long I was asleep, but it must have been long enough for Kano to worry because he was standing above us with a weapon strapped to his side. He's still dressed in the battle leathers he wore for our *r̈ u̥ṣad'ù*.

"Magnus, stop," I grumble as I lean away from his side. The drake stops his grumbling and closes his eyes once again. The drake even looks menacing in his sleep. The drool dripping from his fang does nothing for his image.

"I thought maybe it had eaten you," Kano teases as I stand from my spot. I ignore the pop of my knees as I brush the poky purple sand off my dress. It's a little worse for wear now.

"Magnus?" I ask in a matching lighthearted tone, "No way. We're best buds now."

Magnus only grumbles, cracking open a single eye to let me know he's not amused. Kano is clearly still on edge, so I step closer to him and away from Magnus, which makes the big dope grumpily wake up. He meanders up behind me even as I go toe-to-toe with Kano, brushing my arms over his chest.

"Where are you going to keep him?" Kano asks, his voice still filled with mirth.

"I think Magnus would make a great lapdog. He can sleep at the foot of our bed," I joke, glancing back at the massive figure behind me.

Magnus is good and trainable, like a dog. He listens and learns quickly. He's attentive and protective. I like the concept of a smaller version of him living in our tiny home by the cliffs.

"I don't think he will fit, My Vera."

"Then, maybe the escape pod. We can move it closer to the cliffside and clean it out. Magnus can sleep in there, like his own little cave. Then, he's close by."

Kano kisses my forehead, ignoring the warning growl behind me, "I think that is a wonderful idea."

I motion for Magnus to follow us, and he's happy to listen, keeping a close eye on Kano even as I dance between them. I'm wired after my nap, and the realization that my *r̈ uṣad'ù* is over, and I can *be* now, and my dancing around makes Kano chuckle.

"It seems as though someone has some excess energy."

I wink in his direction, "All the better for you. It is our wedding night, after all."

His brows seem to raise, his tail flicking impatiently behind him. If Magnus could roll his eyes, I would believe I'd seen it happen.

"And what, My Dear Vera, do humans do on their *wedding* night?" Kano waggles his eyebrows, and I giggle, happiness and zoomies blending together to create the perfect cocktail for all I want to do with my new husband.

In my sexiest voice, I whisper, "I think you know."

I practically run all the way home; Magnus keeps stride with me while Kano follows closely behind. Finally, Magnus beds down beside the front door, hissing a final warning at Kano, who pays it no heed. The moment we are inside, he's on me.

Kano snatches me up before I can reach the door to our bedroom. Spinning me toward him, he wraps my legs around him. His lips come to mine, and a moan springs forth. I can feel him carrying us through the maze of rooms, but I pay the ride no mind, grinding against the hard planes of his stomach. He nips at my bottom lip, and I deepen our kiss.

I'm giddy as Kano twists to tumble back onto the bed beneath me. Leaning up on his elbows, he kisses me again, winding one hand through my hair and exploring my mouth with his tongue. Thoughts of our last romp in the sheets have me hot already, but an even better idea invades my mind. Using both of my hands, I shove Kano down onto the bed. My fingers loosen the latches of his armor, popping them open one by one. With each new inch of bare skin, I kiss his neck, across his pecs, and the ridges of his stomach. His groan of pleasure radiates around me when I reach his pants.

I kiss the skin where his waist meets his pants and run my hands up his thighs. Kano watches my fingers slowly work the laces of his pants. When his eyes flick to mine, I can tell he's ready to pounce, but I shake my head. His hands fist in the sheets, but he stays still, watching my every move as I pull his cock free. Finally, I slip from the bed, kneeling between his knees and sizing him up.

It's not like I was a prude on Earth, but there was never anyone of his size. I wasn't sure my usual techniques would work. But the moment I wrap my hands around the base of his cock, my worries are dashed.

"Yes, Vera. Please," Kano groans, his hips shifting slightly in my grip. Running my tongue from the base to the head, I keep my eyes on his, watching them change. The color grows and narrows, and when my tongue swirls the head of his cock it disappears entirely. My body reacts to his pleasure, squeezing my thighs together as I work his cock with my hands and mouth.

His noises grow closer and rougher until he unintentionally pumps into my mouth and begs me for more. As the first drop of cum hits my throat, I moan at the mild flavor. It tastes like salt and smoke. But there's too much for me to swallow, and Kano seems to know that. Pulling his cock from my throat, he pumps it into his fist, groaning as his iridescent seed spills across my face and chest. His cheeks darken at the mess he's made of me, and I can't help but smile.

"My Vera, I'm," An aftershock shakes his body, and he groans again. Another unexpected rope of cum drips from his cock. "Sorry."

His face, still dark with heat, he grabs the sheet from the bed, using it to wipe my face. The sight must be so erotic that blood rushes back to his cock, hardening him once again. He makes quick work of his mess, groaning when I lick his cum from my sticky fingers. He groans at the view, his eyes narrowing on me.

When satisfied with his cleanup, he throws me on the bed. His eyes are still narrowed, and his face looks hard.

"Are you mad?" I ask, scooting toward the headboard and away from him.

"No, My Vera," He groans, one hand catching my ankle. He tugs me down the bed toward him, his voice more monster than man, "I'm hungry."

He spreads my legs wide before him, his eyes catalog the vulnerable position of my body. His mouth nips and kisses up both sides of my thighs, his thumb brushing my nipple, teasing me until I feel my own wetness begin to drip. I'm squirming beneath him, begging for more when he finally gives me what I want. I shout his name when his tongue brushes from my entrance to my clit. Whether in punishment or for tradition, Kano toys with my pussy until I've come three times. And only then does he work his way up my body.

"Are you ready, My Vera?" He kisses my hairline.

"My soul." A kiss on my cheek.

"My heart." A kiss on the corner of my mouth.

I nod emphatically, and his cock thrusts into me. This time is different than the first. After gaining my *ĝha*-mark, every nerve-ending seems to fire with each thrust, driving me closer and closer to pleasure. It's like our *jisa* coalesce into one, and all his fun becomes my own. I can feel each tremor of his pleasure as my walls flex around his cock. As he bottoms out inside me, the bumps above his cock brush my clit. A moan tumbles from my lips in sync with his own sounds of pleasure. I lift my hips to meet each thrust, feeling his stiff cock slide across my G-spot over and over.

I watch the muscles of his stomach flex as he pushes himself into me again and again. His eyes are on mine, and I meet his stare. My lips are parted, panting in breaths as he moves over me. My thighs squeeze around his hips, drawing me closer. The color drains from his eyes again, and he shouts my name as we crash over the edge together.

Kano doesn't try to force me to cuddle this time. Instead, he carries me to the bathing room, gently cleaning my body in a steamy, natural pool of water. He uses soap that smells like berries, watching it bubble over my skin. Then, he cups water in his big hands, dripping it over the soapy skin and watching the bubbles fall away. He lets me finish cleaning and dressing while he fixes the bed. Then, we cuddle until we fall asleep.

I wake up in Kano's arms, and just like that, I have the happily ever after I never dared dream of. Late into my thirties, I married an honorable man. A leader of his people. He gave me everything I could have ever wished for and more. I gambled for some space tickets and won a much bigger prize.

EPILOGUE: CHAPTER FORTY-FIVE

Roxie

Sixteen bullets. I had twenty-four to start, twelve in each magazine. From the first magazine, six bounced off the monster infestation of the *SS Herculean*. One managed to pop out an eye. One killed that chasm creature. That left me with three in the magazine, one in the chamber, and sixteen bullets in total. I check my chamber for the third time tonight, contemplating shooting them into the sky. From how the situation seems, I may never need to fight again if we stay on this planet.

"Why do you sit alone? The night is unsafe." A deep, familiar voice rumbles behind me. The fact that my gun isn't pulled and pointed proves my weakening instincts, but I don't draw it. I'm pretty sure I know who it is sneaking up on me tonight. A glance over my shoulder confirms Kethi Rogeshu. The alien dude from Valkarra.

He's an interesting specimen. Different than Kano in about a hundred different ways. Where Kano is primarily shades of green, Kethi is blue and white like all the shades of a snow-capped mountain. Kethi doesn't have a tail, but he does have fangs – not the Nosferatu kind, more like True Blood. Though, I've yet to confirm what he might use them for. He's also more regal. Kano carries himself like a warrior priest – always praying to his beloved Baso Sheva and aiding the villagers like he's Jesus. Meanwhile, Kethi holds himself like a King – only speaking to the few important people around him and using his charisma to achieve his needs.

I'm told Kethi is equally as much a warrior as Kano and that if Valkarra and Wupeso were to fight, it would be a challenging war. But the Kethi I've met doesn't seem interested in fighting. Or at least not the kind of fighting a gun would serve.

"Just counting bullets, staring at the sky."

I'm sitting on the ledge of the floating island, staring down at the village's lights below. My legs dangle over the edge, but I'm not worried about falling. Some macho V`òllø man would swoop in and catch me – or it wouldn't be my problem anymore. Kethi sits beside me, bringing the smell of tiger's blood snow cones with him. The distorted sounds of music and laughter reach us here, but they're not loud enough to distract us. Kethi certainly isn't distracted by them.

He's staring right at me as he pulls something from his jacket. That's another oddity about Kethi. His clothes are finer, made of tighter weaves and sharper lines. They don't seem to wrinkle as quickly as the linen clothes of Wupeso.

"*Ur'e gu,*" He offers, holding out a sticky yellow cake. I shake my head. I wasn't allowed sweets growing up, and I can hear my mother's voice whenever I think about eating my feelings. *Sugar is bad for you, Hanii. Bad things won't make you feel good.* Of course, I didn't feel good now, so I didn't see how sugar would help. Kethi merely shrugs, popping the prepared bite into his mouth. He swallows and grins in my direction. "You do not seem happy here, Roxie."

"I'm happy," I defend, my hand tightening on the handle of my gun. I can hear the lack of conviction in my voice, my own flat tone, but I stick to my statement. "I'm happy."

"Who are you trying to convince?" Kethi grins, leaning back on his own hands. It's frustrating that he's handsome, even as an alien. He has those masculine sorts of features that attract women – strong jawline, piercing eyes, obvious muscles. But, then, the less noticeable things attract women like me – thick forearm veins, nap-worthy thighs, and a cocky smile. When all the human women first met him, they were all swoony. Even the ones with soulmates whispered about his handsome face.

Shoving my gun in its holster, I turn to face the infuriating (but handsome) alien enemy. Through gritted teeth, I seethe, "I'm. Happy."

Kethi laughs at this, "I can see that."

I glare in his direction, preparing to leave him alone on the island's edge, but he grabs my wrist. It's not forceful, only a gentle ring of his thumb and forefinger – a plea for a moment of my time. I glance down at his hand warily and then back at him. His eyes twinkle like he's some kind of prince charming. Finally, he says, "If perchance you weren't happy here, or you thought you might be happier elsewhere, I'd love to bring you to Valkarra."

ACKNOWLEDGEMENTS

There are many people I would like to thank when it comes to Vera's Alien Leader, but we will narrow it down to those who made the most difference.

First and foremost, I want to throw thanks out there for all the great sci-fi romance writers for inspiring me and creating a space where books like this can exist.

Next, is my beta babes. Elora and Libby, if it weren't for you, how would I ever know if the spice was good? Libby, thank you for catching all the weird accents along the way. And Elora, thank you for showing me exactly how a reader will react.

I also want to include my bookish artists in this list. Thank you W'ynter (@archetypeofdreams) and Fay for your contributions to the project. I can't wait for fans to enjoy your art.

Finally, I want to thank my husband. Truthfully, writing would be a nightmare without him. Thank you for taking hours out of your evenings to listen to me plot and read and spiral over the feedback I didn't want to hear. Thanks for supporting me in every way.

Last but certainly not least, thank you reader. I hope you enjoyed.

BOOK CLUB DISCUSSION

1. How did you feel about the dynamic between Vera and Kano as fated mates? Did their connection feel believable and emotionally satisfying?

2. Poker plays a significant role in the book. How did the author incorporate the game into the story, and what did it symbolize or represent for the characters?

3. The book explores the theme of refuge and finding a home in unexpected places. Discuss the significance of Shojo as a refuge for both Vera and Kano. How did their experiences on the planet shape their characters and relationship?

4. Discuss the secondary characters in the book, such as the other survivors of the SS Herculean EP3 and the inhabitants of Shojo. Which characters stood out to you, and why? Did they contribute to the overall narrative in meaningful ways?

5. The lengths that Kano goes through to protect and keep Vera are a significant part of the story. How did you feel about the conflict and tension that arises from their circumstances? Did it add depth to their relationship, or did it feel contrived?

Thank you for reading "Vera's Alien Leader"! If you've enjoyed the book and would like to stay connected, here are some ways to do so:

Visit MadisonValePublishing.com

Sign up for our mailing list to receive exclusive content, book recommendations, and notifications about new releases directly in your inbox. Stay in the loop and be among the first to know about any exciting developments.

Follow @madi.vale on Instagram

Consider leaving a review of "Vera's Alien Leader" on platforms such as Goodreads, Amazon, or other book review websites.